*W*hat the critics are saying...

Now and Forever

Five Stars! "NOW & FOREVER is a time-travel story that entertained me with a lot of great plot elements; a believable historical backdrop...The fiery, sexual stares that Christian and Alexandria share are very sensual and later, their passionate love scene burns up the pages." ~ *Just Erotic Romance Reviews*

Five Hearts "...This was a great mystery, a beautiful love story and a lot of fun to read. Highly recommended!" ~ *The Romance Studio*

Blue Ribbon Rating: 5 "Julia Templeton has created a superb historical that has everything. A mystery to solve, a time-traveling modern vivacious heroine thrust back in time to solve that mystery and to save the surviving brother who is absolutely scrumptious. The growing love between Alex and Christian is passionate and sensual and decidedly steamy." ~ *Romance Junkies*

"Now and Forever is a quick and highly enjoyable time travel erotic romance with paranormal and suspense elements." ~ *The Road to Romance*

Tears of Amun

"Ms Summers did a wonderful job, even in so few pages. That first scene when they meet, they don't even go to bed yet and it already steams up the screen. A short, but supremely sensual read." ~ *Mon-Boudoir*

"Tears of Amun is a great time travel story. It had a little of everything I love. A lost love, a happy ever after and it's about Egypt. There are some very hot scenes in this story. Who would have thought that they could do that on a moving chariot? The reader will love the romance between Charlotte and Ahmose. If you like time travel, this is the one for you." ~ *In the Library Reviews.*

"The Tears of Amun is a quick, stimulating read. The details and descriptions of ancient Egypt are both interesting and informative. The love scenes are hot, and the pace moves very quickly. Jordan Summers does a fabulous job weaving fantasy elements in with romance and keeping the reader involved during every page." ~ *Romance Junkies*

"I enjoyed this read, it was swift, and yet unhurried. Ms. Summers did a fine job of creating a hero who worships his new love, for this reader; it just doesn't get any sexier than that." ~ *A Romance Review*

THE TEARS OF AMUN by Jordan Summers is a quick, highly entertaining short story that will transport readers back to a mythic civilization full of love, legend and erotic love scenes. A humorous and sexy read, TEARS OF AMUN by Jordan Summers is the perfect book to read when you don't have much time to spare, but are in the mood for a laugh and entertaining dirty thoughts. ~ *Romance Reviews Today*

JULIA TEMPLETON
JORDAN SUMMERS

SOMEWHERE IN *Time*

ELLORA'S CAVE
ROMANTICA PUBLISHING

An Ellora's Cave Romantica Publication

www.ellorascave.com

Somewhere in Time

ISBN # 1419953362

Trade paperback Publication March 2006

Warning:

The following material contains graphic sexual content meant for mature readers. *Somewhere in Time* has been rated *E-rotic* by a minimum of three independent reviewers.

Ellora's Cave Publishing offers three levels of Romantica™ reading entertainment: S (S-ensuous), E (E-rotic), and X (X-treme).

S-*ensuous* love scenes are explicit and leave nothing to the imagination.

E-*rotic* love scenes are explicit, leave nothing to the imagination, and are high in volume per the overall word count. In addition, some E-rated titles might contain fantasy material that some readers find objectionable, such as bondage, submission, same sex encounters, forced seductions, etc. E-rated titles are the most graphic titles we carry; it is common, for instance, for an author to use words such as "fucking", "cock", "pussy", etc., within their work of literature.

X-*treme* titles differ from E-rated titles only in plot premise and storyline execution. Unlike E-rated titles, stories designated with the letter X tend to contain controversial subject matter not for the faint of heart.

*C*ontents

Now and Forever
By Julia Templeton

∞

Prologue

കൗ

Radborne Manor was even creepier than Alex had imagined. The three-story structure was an imposing sight with ivy clinging to its dark gray walls. Pieces of stone lay haphazardly on the ground, surrounded by shards of glass from broken windows. The wrought-iron gate leading to the garden was almost overrun by brush and vines.

No wonder it was rumored to be haunted.

Everything about the place reeked of the supernatural—right down to the large old trees that appeared to have arms for branches.

Alex shook off her misgivings and sank lower into the brush beside the parlor window. Haunted manor or no haunted manor, she had a job to do. Having tracked Frank Consiglio, a prominent London businessman, and his much younger mistress to the abandoned manor, she had precious few minutes to take the pictures and get away before getting caught.

"All right, you cheating pig, smile for the camera," Alex whispered under her breath, focusing in on her client's husband and his bimbo secretary.

This was the part of the job Alex hated most of all—photographing the act itself. With the camera's lens resting on the windowsill, she let out a deep breath and started snapping pictures that would bring her a healthy payday.

After one roll of film instantly rewound, Alex ducked beneath the window and replaced it with another. Placing the finished roll in her pocket, she stood again, camera at the ready—to find a man staring back at her through the lens. Her heart gave a jolt. He was no more than fifteen feet from her, watching her intently.

Alex nearly dropped the camera. Sheer, pulse-pounding panic raced through her. The man who watched her was not the forty-nine year old Mr. Consiglio, but a younger man…maybe in his late twenties or early thirties, and strikingly handsome. His hair was long and dark, his eyes a gunmetal gray. Strangely enough he was dressed in a period costume of snug blue breeches, vest, and a white frilly shirt with billowing sleeves.

He still watched her intently, and seemed to be coming toward her…without moving his feet. When he was a mere five feet away, the sun glinted off an object in his hand. *A knife!* Alex's heart skittered.

He was going to kill her and she couldn't bloody move. Her mind screamed for her to run, but she didn't budge. His eyes held her trapped, mesmerized. She held her breath as he walked straight through the wall…and disappeared into thin air.

Alex fell to her knees, glancing over her shoulder, trying to understand what she had just seen.

The guy had disappeared into thin air!

Her breath caught in her throat. One of Radborne's rumored ghosts? Though she always been skeptical about the supernatural, how could she mistake the vision for anything but a ghost? Especially when said vision walked through walls.

Alex noticed a glimmer of light beside her knee and reached for the object with trembling fingers. When recognized the same blade that the apparition had held, her stomach tightened.

Laughter from inside the manor brought her attention back to the assignment at hand. She wanted just one more roll and she would be on her way — far away from this creepy place.

Slipping the knife in her back pocket, she took a deep breath and tried to concentrate solely on the couple before her. Her hands shook so badly, she'd be lucky if one of the pictures on the roll turned out.

Having gathered ample evidence to give her client, Alex gathered her camera bag and headed for her car, more than ready to leave Radborne Manor and its ghosts. As the first drops of rain fell, she glanced up at the dark, heavy clouds overhead.

Never in all her twenty-seven years had she been so ready to leave a place. She started to jog, but a creeping sense of dread propelled her forward. Legs pumping, heart thumping irregularly, she ran for her car. A horrible sound split the air, stopping her dead in her tracks.

What the hell? The sound came again, a bloodcurdling scream that made the hair on the back of her neck stand on end. Lightning sliced through the air. Before the light dimmed, a piercing clap of thunder followed and clouds rolled over the manor at an incredible speed.

Several moments passed before she dared move, let alone breathe. Rain pelted against her face, and soon her clothes lay drenched against her skin. *I did not just hear someone scream. It's only my imagination.* Looking over her shoulder at the manor, she half-expected Mr. Consiglio to be on her heels. But there was no one.

The haunting cry rang out a third time, from above. Alex jerked her head up as flashing light filled the air again, illuminating a dark-haired man dressed in black standing on the manor roof. When a scream tore from his lungs as though he were daring the greater force to knock him down, her heart skittered.

A second later a bright blaze struck the roof with a hiss, leaving steam in its wake. When it lifted, he was gone.

Alex stood dumbfounded, blinking repeatedly. Was she losing her mind? She ran an unsteady hand down her face. The man on the roof *had* disappeared into thin air—she was sure of it.

Without another thought she raced for her car. Alex rounded the hedge where it was hidden—and halted. A cold knot formed in her stomach. Standing in front of her Peugeot, arms crossed over his chest, was the same man who had been on the roof seconds before. It was impossible for any human to move that fast, which could only mean one thing…he wasn't human.

He made no move toward her, but instead watched her with eyes as blue as the sky and as intense as a predator's. She choked back a cry and took in his handsome features. Long dark hair fell a few inches past his broad shoulders. His shirt clung to his powerful upper body that strained against the wet material. Her gaze shifted lower to dark pants that molded against narrow hips and muscular thighs, and a package that would make any woman smile. Swallowing past the lump in her throat, she ripped her gaze back to his face to find him still watching her with an implacable expression that made her uneasy. What did he want from her?

Beckoning her with a raised hand, he whispered, "Come to me, Alexandria." The words were so soft she thought it might be the wind. "Alexandria," he repeated, his voice stronger, more commanding.

She gasped. It was impossible! How could he know her name when she'd never even met the man?

Yet as their eyes locked, there was something about him that was undeniably familiar. Before she could stop herself, she reached out to him, needing to touch him, drawn to him by a force she couldn't control.

Despite the fact his long-fingered hand was as cold as marble, his touch was electric. As his hand encompassed her own, a current moved from his fingers to hers, then up her arm, until it consumed all of her.

Chapter One

ജ

Alexandria smiled, remembering the gorgeous man, or *ghost*, she had dreamed about last night. Stretching, she opened her eyes slowly, then froze as she caught sight of a tall, broad-shouldered man standing by the window with his back to her.

Uneasiness worked its way up her spine when the man at the window slowly turned to face her. "Holy Mother of God!" The air left her lungs in a rush, as she stared straight into a pair of familiar blue eyes.

A dark brow shot up along with the curve of his lip. "I can assure you, I am not the Virgin Mary," he said in a low, steady voice.

Alex closed her eyes. When she opened them again, maybe he'd be gone.

No such luck. The man before her was none other than the one who'd taken her hand at Radborne Manor during the storm, and now he was watching her with a strange expression.

Coming to her feet, she waited expectantly for his sign of recognition, but he continued to stare. Silent seconds passed before he came toward her in long strides, his stern expression set in stone.

When he stood before her, she poked his chest with her index finger, to find that he, in fact, was real. His eyes flashed with icy contempt.

Looking past his shoulder, she caught a brief glance of an older man walking out the door. Her stomach sank when he closed it behind him with a thud. A click echoed throughout the room. *Great, he'd locked it as well.*

"Who are you?" the handsome man asked, his voice dangerously soft.

She frowned, clearly remembering he had called her by name earlier. "Alexandria."

The nerve ticked in his jaw. "Your given name."

"Alexandria Drake. Who are you?"

"Strathmore."

Strathmore? An odd name, but then again, should she be surprised? Anyone who ran around in seriously out-of-date pants, black knee-high boots, and a pirate shirt was bound to be a little on the bizarre side. Alex bit her lip as she looked around the unfamiliar room, searching for answers. Yet nothing in the pastel-colored parlor full of impressive furnishings and artwork supplied clues. "Where am I?" she asked, trying to make sense of how she'd gotten there.

He walked toward the window, glanced out. He had such nice broad shoulders, an incredible ass, and long, muscular legs. When he turned his attention back to her, her gaze returned to his. "I am finished playing games, Miss Drake."

Alex stared at him incredulously. "I'm playing games? You're the…" She let the accusation die. The last time she'd seen him she had been leaving Radborne Manor. This elaborate room could not possibly be part of the creepy, abandoned manor. So…if she wasn't at Radborne Manor, then where was she? Pushing away the misgivings that threatened to control her emotions, she lifted her chin and met his stare without flinching.

There was a lethal calmness to his eyes. Try as she might, she couldn't think of a legitimate reason why she should be in this strange man's home. Unless he'd brought her here with the intention of hurting her…or worse, killing her.

A warning voice whispered in her head. What if Mr. Consiglio had seen her taking pictures and this was one of his henchmen sent to interrogate her? Her stomach clenched at the thought. Maybe she was in Consiglio's house right now! That would make it awfully convenient to dispose of her and any evidence she'd obtained.

Damn, she'd known the job was dangerous when she'd taken it. But the money had been too good to pass up.

She was in way over her head. Spying an ornate candelabra on a nearby table, Alex backed up. She would have only one chance, so she'd better make it count.

"I would not even attempt it, Miss Drake." His words were as cool and clear as ice water.

Damn it! She dropped her hand to her side and met his gaze. "All right, I needed the money. The man's a cheating pig anyway. It's not like they weren't headed for divorce court as it is."

The man frowned. "What?"

"Consiglio. Obviously that's what this is all about. By the way, where's my camera?" She glanced back over her shoulder at the bed, hoping to find the state-of-the-art Olympus on the nightstand. That camera had cost her a small fortune, and she didn't have the money to replace it. "If you just let me go, I'll give you the film. I promise."

His blue eyes stared relentlessly into her own. "Who is this Consiglio you speak of?"

It was strange, but she had the impression he had no idea what she was talking about…which meant if he was telling the truth, then he hadn't brought her here because of Consiglio, but for something else.

Fear raced up her spine. She took a step back.

He took a step forward. "You have nothing to say?" His head turned slightly as he watched her through the longest, thickest lashes she'd ever seen on a man. "Nothing to say in your defense?"

Afraid she would only make things worse for herself, Alex clamped her lips together.

Shaking his head, he took her by the arm and marched her toward the fireplace. Alex's eyes widened when he pushed open a panel and pulled her through a hidden doorway into a dark corridor.

"What are you doing? Where are you taking me?" She tried to wrench her arm free of his death grip, but she couldn't pull away. Panic overriding reason, she kicked him hard in the shin. He cursed under his breath, but kept pulling her along with him.

Alex fought to contain her growing fear as they started down an unlit stairway. The air grew stale and cold air enveloped her, sending shivers through her entire body. When her feet once again touched flat ground, he released her abruptly.

In the darkness she heard his footsteps walking away from her. She knew she should run and try to escape, but she found herself unable to move, terrified at the overwhelming suffocating feeling that enveloped her.

She had suffered from claustrophobia most of her life—from the time she was three, when she'd broken her mother's favorite vase by accident. By way of punishment, her mother put her in the warm, musty pantry—a small room with no windows and a door that latched. Even now she remembered how stifling the air had been. An hour had seemed like an eternity. Seeing how effective the punishment was, her mother made a habit of throwing Alex in the pantry for the slightest offense.

Light filled the space, bringing Alex back to the present. The man emerged from behind a door with a lit torch in hand. With a quick glance, Alex took in her surroundings. They stood outside a small room with wooden barrels scattered about and a cot in one corner. The room looked suspiciously like a cell. A cold knot formed in her stomach as a scene from *Silence of the Lambs* flashed through her mind.

Spinning around, she raced toward the steps, but he grabbed hold of her arm and brought her up against his hard length.

"You're not going anywhere."

Forcing an iron control she did not feel, Alex kept her tone calm. "You've got to be joking."

"Do not question me," he warned, hauling her toward the cell.

She planted her feet, forcing him to pull her. When she fell to the ground, he resorted to dragging her. Bracing herself against the doorway, she tried to force her confusion into order. "I don't know what kind of sicko you are, but let me tell you right now, I've taken more than five years of karate, and if you try to put me in that cell, you'll pay for it dearly."

The lie fell on deaf ears as he lifted her effortlessly and dropped her to her feet in the cell.

He shut the door between them and turned the key in the lock, and panic quickly rose to the surface. "Do not leave me in here! I can't handle enclosed places. I'll freak out. Do what you will with me, but don't leave me locked up down here."

Her pleading fell on deaf ears. Hearing his retreating steps she pounded on the door with her fists, and screamed, "Let me out of here right now!"

* * * * *

Christian let out a sigh as he settled into his bath. He was so damned tired. He attributed part of his fatigue from having to fight with the hellcat down in the cellar, but also from his lack of sleep. He couldn't remember the last time he had slept through the night. Other than a couple minutes of rest here and there, he spent the better part of the night tossing and turning beneath the sheets, fighting against the nightmares that kept him awake.

It had been that way since his brother's death. Every time he closed his eyes, Devon's face would appear, and the questions surrounding his death would torture Christian, making it impossible to concentrate on anything else, save for his need for revenge.

It would probably get better in time, but it had been four weeks since his brother's death, and still he had no answers to the questions that raced through his mind nearly every moment of the day.

But perhaps he would find some of what he sought by way of the woman in his cellar. Perhaps she was the person who had fled the manor that ill-fated night. After all, she had been found with Devon's missing knife in her pocket.

Yet, she acted innocent of any wrongdoing.

It would take time, but he was determined to get to the bottom of her presence here. Though he knew throwing her in his cellar was medieval, he hoped the time alone would loosen her tongue.

With her unusual mode of dress, and strange manner of speech, it was as though she had fallen out of the sky.

He still could not understand why she was dressed in those strange blue breeches, ugly black shirt, and men's boots. From her clothing to her speech, he had never seen anyone quite like her before. She even wore her hair strangely. The auburn tresses were pulled up high on the back of her head, the length hanging loosely over the tops of her breasts. And what nice breasts they were — a perfect handful, no doubt tipped by rose-colored nipples. The thought stirred his blood, reminding him of the fact he'd been without a woman for over a month, a veritable record for him. Alexandria would be a firebrand in bed — of that he had little doubt.

The side of his mouth lifted recalling her anger. The way her almond-shaped green eyes shot daggers at him. Such haunting eyes.

She truly was a mystery. He thought back over their conversation, when she'd asked for her camera, something about film, and then this Mr. Consiglio. He made a mental list of all his friends and acquaintances. No Consiglio came to mind.

He let out a sigh and sank further into the warm water, resting his head along the tub's edge. The door opened with a creak, then Jared set a glass beside him, and left just as quickly as he'd entered.

With a soapy hand, Christian reached for the much-needed Madeira and drained it in a single motion. Holding the goblet up, he studied the family heirloom that at one time belonged to his great-great-grandfather. The thick, heavy crystal had been handcrafted over a century ago. He remembered Devon drinking from it often…even the night of his death, toasting his friends' good health.

Gripping the crystal stem until his knuckles turned white, Christian closed his eyes against the pain of losing his only sibling. Before he could stop himself, he hurled the treasured antique, cursing as it hit the fireplace and shattered into a thousand tiny pieces.

Tears burned the back of his eyes. His loneliness and regret were as strong now as they had been the night Devon died. Grief was like a stone in the pit of his stomach, and he wondered if he would ever again be the same. If only he could turn back the hands of time…if only it could have been him instead.

There wouldn't be a day, or even a moment, when he didn't see the image of his brother lying impaled upon the wrought iron fence, after he had fallen to his death from the third floor balcony outside his bedchamber. Christian flinched at the gruesome memory. Never would he forget those familiar gray eyes staring back at him so lifelessly, in a face so incredibly pale.

At that moment Christian had become the Earl of Strathmore. And Devon, his older brother by a mere ten months, was dead at the age of thirty.

Rumors had circulated. Christian had heard them via his solicitor.

Who had pushed Devon from the balcony to his death? Who would do such a thing? A title and wealth could cause a person to do strange things in order to get what they wanted—even commit murder. Had Christian pushed his brother to his death? After all, no one could account for Christian's presence when the cry sounded just moments after Devon had been discovered…

"My lord, will you be taking your dinner downstairs this evening?"

Christian looked up with a start, wondering not for the first time if his loyal valet could read his thoughts. Grateful for the interruption, he took the towel Jared offered. "No, I'll be taking it in the study." Rising from the tub, he wrapped it around his hips. "But first, I'm going to have another talk with our guest."

* * * * *

Sitting in the darkness of the cellar, Alex tried to hold back the hysteria threatening to overwhelm her. From the moment she heard him walking away, she sat down on the old cot, closed her eyes, and thought of wide-open spaces. She had to stay calm or she was going to lose it, and it wouldn't be pretty.

Releasing an unsteady breath, she wondered what kind of sick joke this was. Did Strathmore work for Consiglio? If not, then who the hell was this Strathmore? And why her? Some sick abduction fantasy?

Or, easier to deal with, maybe this wasn't even his house? Maybe he was an actor? More than once it had occurred to her that Liz, her friend and business partner, might have put together the whole thing as a practical joke, especially since she had been just a little too gung-ho about Alex taking the Consiglio case. But still…Liz wouldn't be so cruel as to have the man throw her in a cell, since she knew Alex's claustrophobia all too well.

Footsteps outside the room brought Alex out of her thoughts and to her feet. A grating noise came from the other side of the door seconds before it burst open. She squinted as a dim light flooded in from the hallway. Strathmore stood before her dressed in knee-high black boots, snug navy pants, a white frilly shirt, and a navy waistcoat with shards of silver running throughout. His wet hair was worn in a ponytail, drawing more emphasis to his finely chiseled features.

Alex raised an eyebrow at his strange attire, but bit back any remark. She had to admit that despite the fact he was a complete fashion reject and incredibly eccentric, he was also drop-dead gorgeous. The man radiated a vitality that drew her like a magnet. She'd been so furious with him earlier that she hadn't been able to see beyond his accusations. But now he appeared calm, watching her warily with those intense blue eyes. And such sexy eyes they were, fringed by thick, long lashes. His lips curved into a hesitant smile, and she was acutely reminded of her three long years of celibacy.

She pinched her wrist. Sex *should* be the last thing on her mind. First things first. She had to get out of this blasted room.

Straightening to her full height of five feet, five inches, she cleared her throat. Squaring her shoulders, she planted her hands on her hips. "I demand you release me right now. If you don't, I'll have you slapped with a lawsuit so huge, you'll not only lose your home, you'll lose the very clothes on your back!" She held her chin erect, meeting his intense gaze without flinching.

"Are you the one?" he asked in a low voice. He stepped into the light, but his expression remained difficult to read. "Answer me, Miss Drake, are you the one?"

"The one?" she repeated, then cringed when her words brought an infuriated groan from his lips.

Pulling a dagger from the band of his breeches, he closed the distance between them in seconds. Standing so close she could feel the heat of his breath on her cheek, he held the knife inches from her face. "Does this look familiar to you?"

Recognizing the dagger she'd taken from Radborne Manor, she swallowed the lump that had lodged in her throat. She weighed her choices of either telling the truth or lying and decided that given his present mood, it would be in her best interest to lie. "I've never seen it before in my life."

She could literally see his muscles flex beneath the fabric of his shirt. He turned his back on her, putting distance between them before facing her again. "Of course you would deny it." His lethal tone matched his expression perfectly.

Alex thought he was going to leave her again, when abruptly he turned and strode toward her. The next thing she knew, he held the cold blade pressed against her throat. "You've never seen it before, yet it was found in your possession. Who are you, who sent you, and why are you dressed like that?"

As she stared into his cold, stormy eyes, sheer terror swept through her. He *would* kill her—of that she had little doubt. Taking a deep breath, she tried to relax, but found it impossible. Her locked knees threatened to give out, so she replied with more gusto than she felt, "I'm not going to answer any questions until I speak with my attorney."

His glare burned through her, as with a curse he thrust the knife into the wood beam by her ear. Swallowing hard, she lifted her chin and boldly met his gaze, which demanded a quick answer. "Oh, all right! I found the knife just before…well, today, but I only took it for protection. I swear."

The silence lay heavy between them as he watched her without blinking. "I'm sorry I took it. Here, it's all yours." She pointed to the embedded knife, not foolish enough to hand it to him.

His eyes shone brightly in the dark room. They were so penetrating she shuddered involuntarily. "I have questions that need answers, and I expect you to comply. Now, we will begin again."

She lifted her chin.

"What were you doing on my property, why were you carrying the dagger, and why are you dressed like a man?"

"Dressed like a man?" She frowned, looking down at her sweatshirt, jeans, and army boots, all of which were appropriate attire for a stakeout. Sure, some people could call it a rather masculine look, but *dressed like a man* was a bit extreme. And who was he to comment on her attire? At least *she* was in style.

"Aren't you being a bit critical considering…" She lifted a brow as her gaze raked him from head to toe and back again.

Obviously it was not the response he was after. With a growl, he lifted her and hoisted her over a shoulder. When his strong arm tightened over her kicking legs, she pounded her hands into the hard flesh of his back. With every step up the dark stairwell, her teeth rattled and her fury grew.

He threw open a door, then dropped her on the floor at his feet. Her butt stung from the impact, but it was nothing compared to her anger that had passed the boiling point. Coming quickly to her feet, she met his cold stare. If this was a practical joke and he was an actor, he was taking his part a little too seriously. If he worked for Consiglio, she would charge him with kidnapping and assault. She could picture this pretty boy in jail, surrounded by big, burly men, who would just love to have him as a cellmate.

He cleared his throat, reminding her she hadn't answered his question.

She bit down hard on her lower lip and forced herself to remain silent.

"Why don't you just admit it?" he asked, as a slow sardonic smile came to his lips — one she longed to slap clean off his face.

"Admit what?" she demanded, frustrated. She felt like she was boxing an invisible opponent in the dark. *For the love of God — when would this guy get it!* "Just what is it that you think I've done?"

"Where was it you said you were from?" His voice though softer, held an ominous undertone.

Tempted to remain silent, she saw the nerve flinch in his jaw and decided against yet another conflict. "London."

His mouth dipped into an even deeper frown. "Where in London?"

"Fifty-two…" *What was she doing?* This guy had kidnapped her, and held a knife to her throat. If she escaped, she would have him waiting on her doorstep—or worse—in her bedroom closet. "Drury Lane," she blurted.

"Drury Lane?"

Alex nodded, becoming increasingly uneasy under his scrutiny. What would he do to her when he discovered her lie?

Glancing past her shoulder, he ordered, "Michael, check on it."

She turned in time to see a young man leave out the back door. Her gaze swept over at least a dozen people who sat in a large kitchen eating their meal, or had been, until the interruption. They stared at her with open curiosity. Dressed in period clothes, they appeared to take their parts seriously. In fact, they were quite convincing with their looks and gasps of surprise. She took a deep breath and released it. "Okay, this is getting old fast. Maybe you're all part of a reenactment gone wrong. I mean, you've all done a spectacular acting job, but I don't get paid enough for this. I'm very tired and I just want to go home. In fact, I'm going to be on my way."

Before she took two steps, Strathmore caught her wrist in a vise-like grip.

"Jared, see that Miss Drake is kept under lock and key. If she decides to recall anything, I'll be happy to listen. Until then, I have business to attend to." Although he spoke to the servant, Strathmore kept his gaze directed at her, letting her know that in no uncertain terms had he finished with her.

Enough was enough, Alex decided. She'd endured much more than she'd thought possible, and now she wouldn't take it anymore. She tried to jerk away from him, but he held fast. "Listen, buddy, if you think I'm setting foot in that cellar again, you are sadly mistaken."

He was daring her with eyes so light, that one moment they looked translucent; the next so dark, they appeared fathomless.

Refusing to be intimidated, she added, "I'm onto your little game, and I'm sick of it. I haven't seen any of you before, nor, to be perfectly honest, do I ever want to see you again. For something that's meant to be a joke, you are taking this way too far." She lifted her chin another inch and stared into blazing blue eyes. "You will step aside while I walk out that door or I swear I'll make you sorry you ever laid eyes on me." Her gaze fell to his heaving chest. What she wouldn't give to tie him to a chair while she plucked out every damn hair that adorned those well-defined pecs of his.

He surprised her when he abruptly dropped her hand as though it burned his fingers.

"*Sorry?*" His voice hardened ruthlessly. "Oh, believe me, I am sorry. I'm sorry I didn't stop you before you pushed my brother to his death." His eyes narrowed dangerously. "We are all aware that you were involved in Devon's murder. Since I know your secret, why don't you tell me why you've come back to Radborne Manor?" He lifted a dark brow. "Tell me, Miss Drake…did you come back to kill me as well?"

Chapter Two

ಬಾ

Murder?

Strathmore was accusing *her* of killing his brother? Alex stared at the man's retreating back with mouth wide open, too stunned by his accusation to defend herself. As the door slammed shut behind him, her heart slammed against her ribs.

The man was crazy! She turned to the others for some kind of understanding, but they stared back at her in alarm before scattering.

Once the room emptied, Jared, the old servant, moved toward her. She took a quick step back. "I don't need any help!"

Feeling like an unwilling participant in a reality show gone wrong, her mind reeled as she waited for Liz to step out and shout 'surprise!' Yet as the seconds ticked by a sense of foreboding washed over her and panic took control. Seeing the back door slightly ajar, she made a quick decision and ran toward it.

The massive door was heavier than it looked, but fear and the rush of adrenaline gave her the strength to pull it open. Jumping down the steps, she sprinted across the hard ground, her heart pumping so loud it was a roar that filled her ears.

Hurdling over the hedges in the garden, she rounded the manor, ignoring the shocked gardeners she raced past. Daring a glance back, she saw Jared had pursued her, but was quickly losing ground, his age taking a toll. She felt a sense of jubilation knowing freedom was close.

Until she saw *him.*

Her heart plummeted. Strathmore ran toward her with the speed of a panther and a look of raw determination. She screamed at the top of her lungs, lengthening her strides, praying she wouldn't lose her footing and end up rolling head over heels.

He was closing in on her. His boots thundered on the hard ground behind her. With a sharp right turn, she darted through the trees, onto the grass.

Shit! His breathing was loud, right on her heels! A second later he grabbed her by the back of her shirt, and they went toppling to the ground.

Before she could draw breath, he rolled her onto her back and straddled her hips. With one hand he held her wrists above her head; the other pressed against her throat. She took a deep breath — not the easiest task when two hundred pounds of muscle pinned her down and a large hand encircled her throat.

Angry eyes blazed into hers. "I don't know who you are, where you came from, or where you came by my brother's knife, but know this…until such time as your true identity becomes known to me, you will not leave. Do you understand?"

She heard little of what he said, finding it hard to concentrate when she was acutely aware of his lean, muscular body. His tight ass and that part of her that hadn't seen action for three years were in direct contact, and her traitorous body was responding. She glanced at his impressive package, shifted her hips a little and had to swallow the moan that came to her lips. He would be an excellent lover. What she wouldn't give for —

The hand that had been at her throat moved downward. Instantly her nipples snapped to attention, puckering into tight nubs. His gaze lingered on her face, then traveled slowly down her neck to her heaving chest. The side of his mouth lifted, a second before his hand covered her breast.

Alex gasped as he cupped her. It had been far too long since she'd been touched by a man, and it felt wonderful. His large hands encompassing her breasts, his fingers toying with her nipples, pulling them, sending a flood of need throughout her oversensitive body. What if he bent his head, kissed her sensitive breasts, his tongue stroking her—"You have gorgeous breasts, Alex," he said, his voice low and dangerous.

Through her wicked thoughts came a moment of clarity. Horrified at her body's response to him, she turned to the side, trying to buck him off. He braced his legs, and didn't budge—not even the hand at her breast.

Bending over her, his lips traveled from her ear to the wild pulse beating in her neck. Dear God, why did he have to feel so good?

"Did he tire of you?" he whispered softly against her ear as he teased her nipple with finger and thumb. Alex lay still, trembling from a mixture of fear and excitement. "Is that why you killed him, because he grew weary of you and didn't want you anymore? What are you, a scullery maid? Did you think you'd found your prince?" His face was mere inches from hers. Lines of tension around his eyes and mouth marred that gorgeous face.

"My lord!" Jared yelled from behind them.

Strathmore removed his hand from her breast, a wicked smile lit his face, obviously pleased to see her body had responded to his touch. "Why are you here?"

Her mind reeled, and she blurted the first thing that came to mind. "For work."

"Is that what you meant when you said you were not paid enough?" His eyes narrowed. "So, you are indeed a maid?"

She was ready to deny it, but then decided the best course of action would be to just go with it. She nodded.

A moment later she was abruptly pulled to her feet and handed over to Jared who looked out of breath—and furious.

"Jared, take Miss Drake back to the manor and put her to work. It appears that she is in need of employment, and we could always use the extra help."

Without so much as a glance back in her direction, the man who called himself Strathmore headed toward the manor.

* * * * *

Jared held Alex firmly by the arm as though any moment she would run again. It would be worthless to try to escape. So, she walked beside him, listening to his droning voice as he outlined her duties as a maid.

"A maid?" she said aloud, looking to the man beside her for confirmation. But he ignored her, marching forward, his fury evident by the throbbing vein in his forehead. Man, talk about taking a part seriously.

An image of her apartment came to mind. Despite the fact she absolutely hated housework, she did manage to keep a somewhat tidy home. She wasn't sure how good a maid she would make.

A slow smile came to her lips. What was she stressing about? This *had* to be a joke. It was just too far over the top not to be. Plus, Strathmore was too handsome. He was probably some struggling actor who was trying to pay his bills. Liz had done a great job picking him, though. His hair was long and dark, just how Alex liked it. And his features were perfect: strong, masculine, and accented by those gorgeous blue eyes. And that body! All tight, hard, rippling muscle…

She shook her head at her wayward thoughts. Stud or not, did Liz have to get so into it? Sure, Alex had played some good jokes at Liz's expense, but nothing as elaborate as this. It must have cost her a pretty penny to set this one up…but where had the money come from? Alex frowned. She and Liz had started their business less than a year ago, and they lived from one assignment to the next. It seemed they were always broke.

Nothing makes sense, she thought, looking up at the manor.

Her breath left her in a rush.

She stopped dead in her tracks, squinting against the bright sun, wondering if her sight failed her.

She stood in front of Radborne Manor, but *not* the same Radborne Manor she remembered. No ivy clung to the familiar gray stones, nor was the garden gate overrun with brush. Instead, the stones appeared new and the garden gate positively gleamed under the sunlight, an enticing invitation to tour the immaculate gardens that lay beyond.

Terror quickly worked its way up her spine. Frantically, she searched her surroundings and immediately found too many things changed. Her gaze stopped on a man who was putting a new wheel on a black sleek carriage with a gold-emblazoned emblem on its door. *A carriage?* Her mind reeled with the truth, even before she asked in an unsteady voice, "What year is it?"

Jared tightened his grip on her arm, one gray brow raised skeptically. "It is the year eighteen hundred and seventeen, as I am certain you are already aware."

She stared at him in astonishment. *Eighteen hundred and seventeen!* Her mind screamed the year over and over again, but no matter how much she wanted to deny it, she knew she'd entered another time. "Wake up," she said out loud, pinching herself as hard as possible. She winced from the sharp pain.

Dear God, she had traveled through time! There was no way the manor could have changed so dramatically over night, or explain why the people were dressed so strangely.

Alex took a deep, calming breath. She had to keep her cool if she was to get through this. There had to be some logical explanation…like reincarnation? She glanced down at her familiar clothes and body. No, she was the same physical person she'd been before.

Time travel!

Her memory returned to the moment outside Radborne Manor when she'd been leaving and Strathmore had appeared and reached for her. When she'd taken his hand she'd felt an electrical charge—and, apparently, it had brought her here, to the year eighteen hundred and seventeen.

She didn't know whether to scream in horror or laugh hysterically. The only thing she was sure of is that she wanted to go home.

She straightened her shoulders. "Okay," she said under her breath. "I'm in the year eighteen hundred and seventeen, which means no electricity, no phones, no cars, no—" Dear God, the list was endless!

An even more horrifying thought followed the previous one. From what little she remembered about the manor's history, she knew the Radborne brothers had been killed in the early nineteenth century, and that the murders had happened within weeks of each other. Her pulse skittered. And *she* was being accused of committing one of the murders!

Her stomach sank to her toes. What if she couldn't convince Strathmore that she had nothing to do with the murder? Didn't they hang people in this century for murder? Or maybe they planned on burning her at the stake…and hadn't she read in history class that they actually cut peoples' hands off for stealing? Her eyes widened in alarm. *The dagger!* Was Strathmore at this moment sharpening an axe? Her hands went numb at the thought.

"Miss Drake, are you all right? You appear pale."

Alex looked up to find Jared watching her with a quizzical expression. No doubt he thought her crazy, and why shouldn't he? Especially when she questioned her own sanity. "What's Strathmore's full name?"

Jared gave her a sidelong glance, then lifted his chin a notch. "His lordship is Christian William Franklin Randolph Radborne, the tenth Earl of Strathmore."

Strathmore was Christian Radborne! It confirmed her worst fears. She had landed right in the thick of things—smack dab in the middle of a double murder. "No way," she whispered aloud. "Impossible."

"I beg your pardon?" Jared asked, but she ignored him.

Climbing the steps, Alex hardly gave the foyer a glance until she noticed a young woman walking toward them. Dressed in a gray and white uniform, she didn't appear too happy to see Alex.

"My name is Mimi. I have been instructed to show you to your quarters," she said in a clipped voice, motioning Alex to follow her.

On the third floor, Jared stopped and watched them a moment before turning in the opposite direction. After winding down several different hallways, Mimi finally stopped and opened a door. Stepping into the small room, immense disappointment filled Alex seeing her new home away from home. The room with its stark, white walls, and scuffed-up wooden floors screamed for a makeover. A full-size bed had been shoved into the corner to make way for the small vanity and wardrobe. For some reason, she had the distinct impression Strathmore had intentionally given her the most claustrophobic room on the premises. There wasn't even a window—it must have served as a closet at one time. She would never be able to sleep in such a confined space. "I need a different room. Preferably one that's bigger and has a window."

Ignoring her, Mimi thrust two gowns into her arms. "These are your uniforms. Wear the gray one for every day. The black would be for special occasions only." With a hand on the doorknob, she eyed Alex warily. "His lordship does not believe in laziness, nor will he tolerate it." Authority rang in her voice. "You will work under my guidance and I will not condone any nonsense."

Alex smiled blandly. "You might as well save your breath, Mimi, because I won't be here long."

Letting out an exasperated breath, Mimi stepped outside the door. "I will see you promptly at six o'clock in the wash room. I do not have to remind you—"

Alex slammed the door shut in the servant's face.

Muttering came from the other side of the door, but Alex ignored it. She had too many other things to worry about…first and foremost, how in the world to get out of this nightmare.

* * * * *

Christian made his way down the stairs, a solitary candle lighting the way. It was two in the morning, and everyone was tucked into their beds, sound asleep.

Everyone, but him. As usual, he was awakened by unwanted dreams. Strangely, the dream hadn't been about Devon, but about the newest servant of Radborne Manor. In the dream Alexandria had come to his room, ordered him onto his back, and then proceeded to straddle him, much as he had done to her that afternoon. Her chemise had ridden up past her hips, and she rubbed her sweet, hot cleft against his hard cock, taunting him. Although he yearned to touch her, he could not move, as though he'd been held down by an invisible force. He smiled at the memory of her rotating hips, torturing him as she lifted the chemise, exposing her firm, ripe breasts. She had positioned herself over his engorged penis, and he had awoken with a start—to find himself alone, with the hardest, thickest erection he'd ever had.

With heart still pounding, he'd wrapped his fingers around his shaft and stroked himself, envisioning her face and what she would look like beneath her clothing. He'd felt her firm breasts, had felt her response to his touch, had seen the desire in her eyes, though she tried to mask it with fury. His strokes increased, his breath quickened, and he grit his teeth as he climaxed, promising himself he'd tame Alexandria Drake soon enough.

He and Alexandria were most definitely *not* finished…

Entering the library, the flame wavered as he crossed by the window and he stopped short, seeing a bulky shape on the settee. As he approached, the person rolled over and the candlelight illuminated the intruder.

Alexandria.

He frowned and ignored the jolt of his heart upon seeing her. Why was she in his library in the middle of the night? What was she up to now?

He took a step closer and watched her, wondering once again about this strange woman who had come storming into his life. Her hair was unbound, making her face appear softer. Her long lashes fanned against cheekbones sprinkled with tiny freckles. How innocent she looked in slumber. How unlike the spirited girl he'd met that day—and the vixen in his wicked dream.

"Who are you, Alexandria?" he asked, his voice barely a whisper.

Her eyes opened, and she smiled sleepily, the gesture making his pulse quicken. She stared at him without blinking, her silky hair all sleep-tousled, her pink, full lips slightly parted. In that moment, she was painfully attractive, more attractive to him than any other woman had ever been.

"I couldn't sleep in my room."

She went upon her elbows and the blanket fell below her breasts, which were outlined by the cotton material of her chemise. She made no move to cover herself. Blood filled his groin and stirred his cock to life once again.

Swallowing a groan, he pulled his gaze back to hers. "Why could you not sleep in your room?"

"For one, there is no window, and no one said anything about sharing a bed with someone else. I about had a heart attack when one of the upstairs maids climbed into bed with me. Mind you, she is not a small woman."

He refrained from smiling and sat down in a nearby chair. He set the candle on the table between them, making sure to keep his gaze from falling beneath her chin. "Let me see if I understand completely. Due to some aversion you suffer from, you must have a window in your room in order to sleep?"

Sitting up, she drew her knees to her chest and tucked the blanket under her toes. "I can't be in enclosed places. I panic. I have to be able to see out. If not, I feel trapped, and well, it's not a pretty sight when I lose it."

"Lose it?"

"Go crazy." She grinned and the smile transformed her into a beauty, complete with large dimples.

He knew he would catch hell from the other servants, but he couldn't resist her. "We'll have to find you another room then, won't we?"

He could see surprise in her face by the way she watched him. And wariness.

"Do I have to share a bed with someone?"

He smiled inwardly. "You have never shared a bed with someone before?" He allowed a hint of double entendre to creep into his voice—a double entendre she clearly understood by the way her brows lifted nearly to her hairline.

Alex sat up straighter. "I *prefer* to sleep alone."

He'd hoped for a different answer entirely. "I will see what I can do then," he said, noticing for the first time the book on the floor beside the settee. He squinted, but could not make out the title in the waning light. "What are you reading?"

Her eyes widened, and she quickly averted her gaze. "Just something from your shelf." Standing, she pushed the book under the settee with a foot. "Hey, do you think I could get a glass of water?"

He stood and took the step that separated them. The pulse in her neck beat in double-time, and he had to resist the urge to touch her soft skin. "What's the matter, Alex?"

"Nothing." It came out a squeak.

"You don't want me to know what you're reading, do you?"

The wariness left her face, replaced by determination. She lifted her chin. "No."

Before she could react, he leaned down and snatched up the book, instantly recognizing it. *The Pleasures of Sex*. A volume full of graphic illustrations a chum from university had given him upon graduation. A book he'd kept in the top drawer of his desk, and not on the shelf as she'd said.

Though his mind was running rampant with the thought of this exquisite creature reading the most scandalous literature he had on the premises, he could not ignore the voice of reason that was all but screaming in his brain. *She has gone through your desk!* No servant would dare such a thing. It seemed all his suspicions had been confirmed, but he would wait before accusing her. "You can read?"

She frowned at him, clearly affronted. "Of course I can read."

Very few servants knew how to read or write.

He ran his index finger over the gold lettering. "An interesting choice of literature."

Her throat convulsed as she swallowed hard. "I found it rather unrealistic."

Unrealistic? "And what may I ask was unrealistic?"

"Some of the positions are so outrageous. I can't imagine standing on my head while—well, I doubt a woman could even—" She grabbed the book from his hand and flipped through the pages. "Like this," she said, thrusting the book at him. "That's realistic?" She snickered. "Yeah, right!"

Christian wasn't sure if he should be shocked by her lack of embarrassment or enthralled by it, and what of her bizarre speech? She stood in front of him in a sheer cotton chemise, her hair disheveled, looking like one of the vixens in the book he held. Except she wasn't standing on her head, naked with…he snapped the book closed.

Alex shifted on her feet, uncomfortable with the change in Radborne's expression. The way he watched her made her aware of how little she was wearing. Not only that, they were comparing notes on a very graphic, very sexual book. Alex would bet her life that he'd tried nearly every one of those positions. She briefly shut her eyes and willed away the unwanted image of him with another woman, trying out all those sexual illustrations.

When the image wouldn't go away, she all but ripped the book from his hands and tossed it on the couch. "I could really use that glass of water."

He cleared his throat. "I shall get it for you then." He had no more said the words and he was out the door. Alex was shocked he didn't tell her to get the water herself. And why didn't he say anything about her getting the book from his desk? They both knew she was guilty of rummaging through it.

Rather than question her good fortune, she took the opportunity to return the book to his desk drawer before he returned. She raced back to the settee and covered every inch of flesh from neck to toe with the blanket.

"Here we are," he said, slipping back into the room as quietly as he had left. His gaze was on the too-full glass, obviously concentrating on not getting any water on the floor. He had probably never retrieved water for anyone, especially a servant. Alex was glad he did now. At least it diverted his attention and gave her the opportunity to stare at him when he was unaware. He truly was a gorgeous man; all tanned skin and dark hair. And those blue eyes framed by long lashes. *Damn!* He gave off a sexual vibe that caused a twinge in her groin—one she felt all the way to her toes, along with a deep ache to feel him inside of her.

"Thank you." The words came out huskier than she would have liked. The side of his mouth lifted slightly as he handed her the glass and sat back down.

"I've been thinking further about the room predicament, and I believe I can find you something more suitable given your phobia."

His lower lip was full, the upper just right. His white teeth matched the white of his shirt exactly.

Suddenly, he stopped talking and watched her with a lifted brow.

"Huh?" she said stupidly, sitting up straight. "Sorry."

"I was saying that tomorrow I shall see to it that you have a new room, one with a window."

He grinned devilishly, and it kicked his looks to a higher level. Who was this guy who was charming and downright likable? Definitely not the intimidating man she'd met earlier today—the same man who had put her in a dark cell and accused her of murdering his brother. "Why are you being so nice to me?" she asked before she could stop herself.

He leaned forward and put his hands together. Alex had thought his hands a nice size when the one had cupped her boob, but she hadn't realized how big they actually were…until now. His fingers were long and tapered, with nice sculptured nails. Masculine hands that would bring a lot of pleasure to a woman. Once again her traitorous thoughts returned to the gutter. She counted to five. *What was her problem?* Just because she hadn't had sex in over three years, didn't mean she had to constantly fantasize about this hot, desirable man in front of her.

"I realized I handled our first meeting badly. I was reacting to finding Devon's knife on you. I did not mean to scare you. Am I forgiven?"

Forgiven? *Was he kidding?* She wanted to be in his good graces. Maybe then she could snag an elevated position—like becoming his mistress. "Of course." Maybe this little adventure wouldn't be so bad after all.

"Thank you," he replied, his gaze dropping down to the tops of her breasts. She had to resist the urge to arch her back just so. With a yawn, he stood. "Well, you had best get to sleep. Morning will be here before we know it."

She nodded in return, watching as he made his way to the door, the light leaving with him. Snuggling into the blanket, Alex told herself to suppress her excitement, because after all, she didn't know which Christian Radborne would show up in the morning—the charmer, or the asshole.

Chapter Three

ॐ

Keeping her back close to the wall, Alex moved quickly down the hallway, creeping past rooms where maids were busy cleaning. In the past two days, she'd found little time to investigate…until now. She made it down one flight of steps, when out of the corner of her eye she caught a movement and heard a door close. She smiled to herself. Someone had just entered the room she had been warned 'under no circumstances' to enter. Mimi had told her just last night that the quarters in the wing had belonged to Devon, and, therefore, were to be left alone. Apparently no one had gone into the room since shortly after his death, nor were they supposed to be there now.

But someone was in there, and her curiosity got the best of her. Alex headed down the hallway, thinking of what she would say to the person who'd gone ahead of her. It had to be a servant, because Christian had left a while ago, and from what Mimi said, he would be gone for hours.

She smiled inwardly recalling the way he'd looked at her last night when he discovered she'd been reading the sexy book. There had been a warmth in his eyes, the slightest curve of his lips as he watched her.

Slowly, she opened the door while glancing over her shoulder. Seeing the way clear, she darted into the room. "Hello?"

The word echoed off the walls.

Pressing her back against the closed door, she scanned the room with a glance and found herself alone. Where was that servant? She *knew* someone had entered.

Her self-assuredness quickly faded as the smell of mildew assailed her. A cold dread seeped into her bones, as she glanced around the room filled with sheet-draped furniture that cast eerie shadows on the walls. She'd made a mistake by entering the creepy room. Spinning around, she grabbed for the doorknob, but before she could open it, a voice behind her said, "Do not be afraid."

She whipped around again, then collapsed against the door with a thud. The man had not been there two seconds ago. Where had he come from? Handsome and familiar, she instantly recalled where she'd last seen him and her mouth dropped open. It had been in her own time at Radborne Manor. He'd been the man with the dagger, who'd walked through the wall.

Her heart pounded in her ears.

"I won't hurt you."

"Who are you?" she asked, her voice squeaking, exposing her uneasiness.

"My name is Devon."

"Devon. As in Devon Radborne?"

He grinned boyishly. "I am one and the same," he replied with a gallant bow.

The resemblance between this man and Christian was too close to be called coincidence. He had the same dark hair, and the same shaped eyes. The only difference appeared to be their eye color. Where Christian's eyes were a striking blue, this man's were a gun metal gray. He was also leaner, and not quite as tall as Christian.

"Don't leave," he said, taking a step closer.

"You're not here. This is my imagination." Her hands shook as badly as her voice. When he moved toward her—or rather floated toward her, his feet inches above the floor—she turned the doorknob behind her back, ready to flee if he so much as moved an inch.

She stared at him, unable to believe her eyes. "How can you do…?" He wasn't human, that's how. Before she could stop herself, she let go of the knob and reached out to touch him. Her hand moved through air. "What *are* you?"

"I could tell you what I am, but then you wouldn't believe me." He grinned mischievously. "Don't fear me, Alex. I've been waiting so long for you."

"How do you know my name?" Uneasy again, she wished she were on the other side of the door, or better yet, home in her own century.

"I know most everything about you. I've been watching you since your arrival." The dimples in his cheeks deepened. "You've caused quite a stir. My brother and his servants are not quite sure what to make of you."

As she stared into his eyes, studying his expression, Alex relaxed. He wasn't going to hurt her.

"Do you believe in life after death, Alex?"

"Life after death?" She pressed her hand tightly to her chest. Did he mean she was dead? She hadn't even considered that. She sucked in a breath. If she was dead, she would never get her house in the country that she'd been saving for. And she'd secretly hoped to have a husband and children.

"In time you will accept it. You have fought it from the start," he said matter-of-factly.

Accept? What was there to accept? Sure, he was dead and he knew it, but she hadn't even realized she'd died. "I'm...I'm dead?"

Amusement flickered in his eyes. "Of course you're not dead."

Closing her eyes, Alex leaned her head back against the door and breathed a sigh of relief. When she opened her eyes again, he was watching her intently. "You said you were waiting for me? How could you have known I was coming?" An important question, but she was not sure she really wanted to know the answer.

"Do you remember in your own time when you came to Radborne Manor? You were outside the library. You saw something besides the two people you were after. You saw me then, didn't you?"

She nodded. "Yes, it was you."

"And you saw Christian as well."

"He was the one on the roof, and the one who met me at my car. He took my hand, and I woke up in another time."

"Yes, remember the knife you found."

"It was yours."

He nodded. "When you took that knife, it sealed your fate. I knew that Christian would recognize it when you came to this time. He would want to find the answers, and he would keep you close."

Hope flooded her at his words. *He* was her link to get back to her own time! Soon she would be back where she belonged—back in her apartment over her office on Drury Lane. "Okay, I'm ready for you to send me back. Do we need to get the knife? It's probably still imbedded in the—"

"I am afraid I can't."

She gave a desperate laugh. "Can't what?"

"Please understand, I cannot send you back," he said, his tone apologetic. "Not until we catch the person who killed me before they murder my brother. When that is accomplished, I will deliver you back to your own time."

She froze at his words. "*We?* What is this *we?* You're asking *me* to help you?" He couldn't be serious. She was a private investigator, but her cases were limited to insurance fraud and cheating spouses. Finding a murderer was a different story altogether. "You do know that your brother thinks I'm the one who killed you?"

"Trust me, if he truly believed you were responsible for my murder, you wouldn't be standing here now." He studied her thoughtfully for a moment, then said in a gentle voice, "Alex, do you believe this is real?" He motioned at the room. "I mean all of it."

She nodded, almost afraid of what he was about to say.

"Yes, Alex, it is real. I have been dead for four months and two days, yet I stand before you...perhaps in spirit, but nonetheless, I am here, and you, Alex, are the only one who can help me now.

"I need your help." The way he said it, made it sound like a plea.

Even if she wanted to, she couldn't deny him his last wish, especially when it was her only chance to leave this century. "I'll think about it."

"Good, that's all I ask."

"It wouldn't hurt to have more data, one way or the other." Alex took a deep breath, her mind racing ahead, trying to recall more about the murder that she'd heard about in grammar school. "First off, I'll need to know the names of the people here that night."

"We were having a masquerade party that evening. There were over two hundred guests in attendance."

"Two hundred guests!" She stared at him incredulously. "How in the world can I find one killer out of more than two hundred suspects, especially when I'm working as a servant?"

How could she possibly pull it off? Sure, if there were a handful of suspects that would be one thing, but two hundred suspects? He'd made a huge error in judgment if he thought her capable.

She ran her hands down her face, feeling not at all up to the challenge.

"Do not doubt your ability, Alex. I trust you implicitly, and I know you'll do everything in your power to help me."

It took her several moments to realize what had happened. She dropped her hands to her sides. "You can read my mind, can't you?"

"Yes, I can." His grin broadened, exposing deep dimples. "Alex, I want you to trust me as much as I trust you. I will help you as much as I can, but it is up to you to see that the murderer is caught before he kills Christian. Though I remember little of that night, I do have one clue. I believe the killer to be a man. I had been alone, standing out on the balcony when I heard someone in my bedchamber. I thought it my valet, but the footfalls were not familiar. I turned, but it was too late. I was shoved hard from behind...and that's the last thing I remember."

And then he had died a horrible death. Alex had the sudden urge to hug him.

He must have read her thoughts again because he looked amused. Suddenly, the smile disappeared and he turned his head sharply to the left as if looking through the wall at something.

"Alexandria!" an angry male voice bellowed from the landing.

Alex jumped. "It's Christian!" When she turned back to Devon, he was gone. "Devon?"

When he didn't respond, Alex took a deep breath and stepped from the room as quietly as she'd entered. Immediately the hallway took on a much brighter hue and warm air surrounded her again. Shutting the door behind her, she almost ran, then she saw Christian standing at the top of the stairs, and her pace slowed considerably.

He stood with one hand on the balustrade, the other firmly planted on his hip. His eyes, as warm as ice, moved down her body.

It seemed the *asshole* had returned.

Why was it every time she saw him her heart would pound nearly out of her chest? And why was he always so moody? Last night she'd thought they had a moment. Hell, he'd actually smiled. Her anger disappeared as she realized *he* was the reason she was here. His life was on the line, and she'd been sent here to save him from certain death.

She must remain calm...and have empathy for the man.

With her back ramrod straight, she went to him and dipped into an exaggerated curtsy. "Your lord."

"My lord," he corrected, his voice softer than expected.

"Yes, *my* lord?"

He still watched her intently, obviously expecting her to wilt under his gaze. "What were you doing down there?" He pointed in the direction of Devon's room.

She glanced over her shoulder at the dark hallway and shrugged. "I was told to clean that wing."

"Not on this floor."

"Are you sure, my lord?"

"Alex, do not play naive with me." A muscle quivered at his jaw. "You have entered quarters which you have been told not to enter."

Unable to defend herself when she was downright guilty, she shifted on her feet and hoped her punishment was not too extreme. "I'm sorry. I…must have gotten lost."

"Well, don't get *lost* again."

She nodded. "I won't."

After a few seconds, he let out an exasperated breath. "Jared is looking for you. I will refrain from telling him where I found you."

"I appreciate that, Strath…my lord."

Was it her imagination or had his eyes softened? And his lips looked on the verge of a genuine smile. For all that he pretended indifference, Alex had a feeling he liked her. She had seen it in his face last night, the way he looked at her. Could he be feeling the attraction too?

She hoped so. It might make things interesting.

His gaze slipped to her lips for a second, before he met her gaze once more. Yes, he was definitely attracted to her.

"Well, you'd better get to work. Oh, and Miss Drake, you may want to change into another gown." The corners of his mouth lifted in an amused smile. "You've cobwebs and dust all over that one."

"I will," she answered in a silky voice she hardly recognized as her own. Flustered by her attraction to him, she quickly sat on the railing and slid down to the floor below.

Jumping off, she looked up and gave him an angelic smile before skipping down the hall.

* * * * *

It was plain and simple—Alex hated Christian's houseguest on sight.

A so-called second cousin, Abigail Duarté had skin as smooth as cream, a tiny nose she held high in the air, pink full lips that could pout just so, and blue almond-shaped eyes that could probably spout tears at the drop of a hat.

In short, the lady was trophy-wife material.

Having spent the last few hours in the kitchen preparing dinner, Alex looked a mess. Now she wished she'd changed into a clean gown like Christian suggested.

Conscious of her stained gown and lopsided ponytail, Alex took in Abigail's perfectly styled hair, the sparkling jewels woven throughout the gold tresses that framed her delicate features.

Alex had never felt so undesirable. Maybe Liz had been right? Maybe a little makeup wouldn't hurt from time to time.

With steady hands, she poured the wine into the crystal glass Abigail held with gloved fingers. Alex had always prided herself on giving people a chance to prove themselves but it was different with Abigail. Her hatred for the woman had been instantaneous.

Abigail sat in the high-backed chair looking like a princess, dressed in ice-blue silk that fit her petite figure like a second skin. Diamonds dripped from her ears, neck, and fingers, reminding Alex again how easy the rich and beautiful people had it in life…no matter what century.

Glancing up, Alex noticed Christian's gaze was focused on her gravy-stained gown. A hint of a smile played at his lips as though he knew she had intentionally not changed just to annoy him. While avoiding eye contact with him, she caught sight of a motion over his shoulder. Her eyes widened in disbelief. Devon stood at the far end of the room, waving at her.

She raised her hand to wave back, but caught herself just in time.

"Watch what you're doing!"

Alex jumped at the sound of Abigail's shrill cry. She groaned inwardly seeing the wine she'd been pouring had spilled over the edge of the woman's glass and onto the white tablecloth.

Abigail stood and threw her napkin on the table. "You fool! Now I'll have to change my dress. Christian, look at what her carelessness has done to my new gown!"

Setting the carafe on the table, Alex bent to inspect the spot on Abigail's gown. It was so tiny, hardly visible. Alex frowned. "It's not that bad."

"What do you know? You are just a clumsy servant," Abigail spat.

"Just a clumsy servant?" Alex clenched her fists at her sides, and bit the inside of her cheek. *Oh, it would be so easy to —*

"Alexandria!" Mimi's voice cut off her malicious thoughts. "Please see me in the kitchen," she said, following Alex through the swinging doors. When they were safely on the other side, Mimi leveled a disapproving frown at her. Alex, you have no right to talk back to her, and even worse, you weren't paying attention to what you were doing." She sighed heavily. "I don't know what to do with you, Alex, I truly don't."

"But you heard her! You're just a clumsy servant!" Alex mimicked. The last thing she needed right now was to get into more trouble. Devon and Christian needed her help. She flashed her best innocent smile. "Doesn't that make you mad, too? After all, she wasn't just talking about me, but all servants in general.

Just because she has money doesn't make her any better than us."

Mimi's dark eyes softened and she even fought a smile. "But you *are* clumsy."

"True," Alex agreed, knowing she'd won the battle. Considering she and Mimi had started off on the wrong foot, the woman was starting to come around, even smiling at Alex from time to time. "But only because I was a little distracted. I'm only human after all, and I'm sure she's made mistakes too. Plus, what right does she have to judge me?"

"All right," Mimi said, holding up a hand. "I understand your anger, but it will not change anything. We are servants. This is what we do, and there are times we have to forgo our pride." She smiled softly and glanced toward the door. "But she is quite a little witch, is she not? Do you know she has her sights set on his lordship? Her brother will be here within the hour. He is hoping to post the banns the moment Christian is out of mourning."

Christian was going to marry his cousin. *Ewwww.* Images of the two thrashing about in bed came unheeded and Alex flinched. Why should she care if Christian was going to marry the bitch? *Because you want him*, a voice in her head responded loud and clear.

The bell rang, signaling Christian or Abigail needed her.

"I'll see what they need. You may bring in the duck," Mimi said, handing the heavy platter to her.

Alex managed to get to the table without falling flat on her face. Abigail scooted away from her—clearly afraid she would once again be careless and perhaps drop the plate in her lap. The woman couldn't possibly know how tempting the idea was.

Moving to Christian's side, Alex set down the platter and kept her gaze focused on her task. Her hand trembled as she tried to dislodge a piece of duck from the serving fork, but the meat wouldn't cooperate. "Come on," she muttered under her breath.

Looking amused, Christian handed her a knife. Conscious of his fingers so close to her own, she dropped the knife, and to her horror, it landed in his lap. Without thinking, she reached down and grabbed for the knife and her fingers brushed over the rigid length of his cock. Swallowing hard, she found the knife and wished for a hole in the floor to open and swallow her. Refusing to look at Christian, she leaned forward and pushed the meat from the fork.

Catching a movement from the corner of her eye, she guessed it was Devon once again making an appearance. This time she was prepared. She smiled in his direction and then quickly looked away. Unfortunately, Christian glanced over his shoulder at the empty room. His brows were raised in question when he turned back to her.

She moaned inwardly. He probably thought she was nuts. "Will there be anything else?"

Their gazes locked, and for a moment she could swear there was a smoldering flame within those blue depths. Did he want her as much as she wanted him? For a moment she let her mind run rampant. What would it be like to feel the corded muscles of his strong back or tight abdomen beneath her fingertips, or to feel the touch of his soft lips against her as they kissed a path down her body? Heat warmed her veins as she envisioned him lifting her hips to his face and kissing her slick folds…his tongue expertly lifting her clit, teasing it relentlessly as he brought her to climax time and again, while she wove her fingers through his thick, dark hair, pulling it, urging him on.

Her gaze locked on his lips, she sighed softly. He would be a marvelous lover, with a stamina that would put most men to shame. She imagined him lying on her bed, wearing nothing but a smile, his long, thick cock reaching up past his navel.

Suddenly the sides of Christian's mouth lifted slightly, and a devilish glow sparkled in his eyes as though he too could read her thoughts. Alex dropped her gaze to the floor as heat flushed her cheeks once again. Geez, could she be any more obvious?

"My lord, will that be all?" Mimi's voice rang out behind Alex, and this time she was thankful for the maid's intervention. Though Alex didn't hear Christian's reply, she did hear Mimi excuse her.

Safely alone in the kitchen, Alex poured herself a glass of the finest wine in Strathmore's personal collection. She really had it bad for Christian. Her fingers still tingled where she'd touched him. Of all places *there*! She was shaking as she tipped the glass to her mouth, and drank. Savoring the wine's flavor, she swirled it around her tongue, enjoying the warmth as it worked its way down to her knotted stomach. Setting the glass on the counter, she let out a sigh.

"Bravo, Alex!"

Alex gasped and turned to find Devon standing beside her. "Are you trying to kill me?"

"So sorry." His amused expression completely contradicted his apology. Taking a seat on the counter, he dangled his long legs over the side. "I never cared for Abigail. Her brother spoils her terribly. She's used to being catered to by all."

Alex hoisted herself up beside him, hoping that no one, namely Jared, walked in to find her slacking off. "I'm surprised Christian would want a woman like her."

"I am not so certain he is interested in Abigail. She had been chasing me up to the time of my death. Truth be told, the night of my death I had disappeared to my bedchamber to have a cigar and escape her advances. "

And now that Devon was dead Abigail wanted the heir.

"Of course Christian knows Abigail's interested in him for his title, but he's never been the kind of man to be held by one woman. In fact, women of the *ton* have been whispering behind their fans for years that Christian is irresistible, unapproachable, and unattainable—qualities that women love I might add."

"Well, I think he can do a lot better than her." Hopefully Devon wasn't as good at reading her mind as she feared.

"Such as yourself?" Devon smiled sardonically, proving he did know she wasn't as immune to his brother's charm as she pretended to be.

"Don't be ridiculous!" Dropping to her feet, Alex rinsed the glass, set it back on the shelf, corked the bottle of wine and set it back where it belonged. With any luck, no one would notice some wine was missing.

Not a moment too soon.

Mimi passed through the swinging door, an irritated frown on her face. "She demands an apology."

"What?" Alex hoped she hadn't heard right.

Mimi shrugged. "I know you don't want to do it, Alex, but I don't see where you have any choice."

Alex turned to Devon for help, but he quickly nodded in Mimi's direction, reminding Alex that she was the only one who could see him.

She sighed, realizing her dilemma for what it was. If she didn't apologize, she'd have Christian to answer to. Yet her pride refused to give in, no matter how much trouble it caused. Alex shook her head. "No way. I won't do it."

Mimi sighed. "Alex, please. She will stand firm until you apologize. People have been released from their position for far less."

Alex always had a hard time saying she was sorry, especially when she wasn't. Her grandparents had called her stubborn and strong-willed, and maybe she was. But just the idea of apologizing to that woman made her nauseous.

She would stick up for herself if it killed her. "Well, it will be a cold day in hell when I apologize to some spoiled little bitch, who expects everyone to run when she snaps—"

"Alexandria," Christian's voice boomed from behind her, cutting her off in mid-sentence.

Chapter Four

ဢ

Plunging her hand into the lukewarm water, Alex smiled as she pictured the bucket of suds flying out the window, straight onto Abigail, who was out walking the gardens with her brother. Reginald was as pretentious as his sister, snapping his fingers whenever he required something. A most annoying habit that made Alex want to give him the finger.

But she couldn't because she was the hired help, and she couldn't risk the chance of being fired.

Sitting back on her heels, she rubbed her red, chapped hands together and looked around Strathmore's bedroom. It screamed of masculinity with its dark colors and deep mahogany furnishings. A thick, plush rug in black and gold covered a good portion of the floor and begged to be stepped on…made love on. She couldn't resist. Taking off her shoes and stockings, Alex walked onto the carpet and sighed. The feel of the rich fibers squishing between her toes couldn't have been more deliciously decadent.

How dark and elegant this room was: so like the man who lived here. She smiled. Last night she'd sensed Christian watching her as she served dinner. More than once she'd looked up and caught him staring, but instead of looking away, he'd met her stare head on.

She knew that look. He liked her, desired her, his eyes dark and heavy-lidded, like he yearned to throw her over his shoulder and haul her to his bedchamber, and make love to her until she couldn't stand. Glancing at the huge bed, she envisioned herself sprawled there, Christian poised above her, his thick cock probing her slick entrance. Her skin prickled at the image, her nipples becoming sensitive, rubbing against the course fabric of her uniform. She shook her head at her wayward thoughts.

She had to quit thinking of Christian sexually. Her focus *should* be on saving him, period.

Focus on your work, she told herself, but a cherrywood box sitting on top of a dresser across the room drew her attention. What kind of jewelry did a man like Christian Radborne wear?

Curiosity got the best of her. She glanced over her shoulder. Seeing no one, she walked over and traced the intricately carved coat of arms in the polished lid with a finger.

With a quick look toward the still closed door, Alex opened the box's lid. Inside lay a pocket watch, rings, and a woman's diamond earring, which she picked up and immediately began searching for the partner. As the seconds ticked away it became evident the earring had no match. Presumably, the woman had lost its partner in Christian's bed. She dropped the earring as though it burned her fingers.

She was ready to close the lid when she spied a small burgundy velvet bag in the deep recesses of the box. Opening it, she poured the ring it held into her palm. Lifting the beautiful feminine ring to the light, she saw that there was an imprint inside the band. But no matter how she turned it, she couldn't make it out.

"Looking for something, Miss Drake?"

Startled, she almost dropped the ring.

Shit! The man seemed to have an uncanny ability to find her at the very worst possible moment.

Heart pounding, she turned to find him standing in the doorway, wearing nothing but a towel that hung low around his narrow hips. She swallowed hard as her gaze worked slowly up his body. His hair was wet and slightly disheveled, the wet strands clinging to his neck and broad shoulders. She cleared her throat. "I…well you see, I thought you were out."

With deliberate slowness, his gaze moved to the cherrywood box, then back to her, his expression clearly accusing. "So while my attention was elsewhere, you thought to go through my things?"

"I…" She couldn't think of anything clever to say and instead simply pointed toward the still open box as though that would explain everything. This was not good. He obviously thought her a thief, and by all accounts, she looked guilty. "I didn't take anything," she blurted. "If you don't believe me, then check for yourself." His intense stare unnerved her. "I…was just curious."

His mouth twisted wryly. "Why is it you are so curious, Alexandria?" His tone was velvet soft. "I have asked myself this question numerous times since your arrival and I have yet to find an answer."

It was hard to concentrate when he stood before her wearing nothing but a towel. Her gaze dipped below his chin to his hard chest, down over the rippling six-pack of his washboard stomach and the solid dark line of hair that disappeared beneath the towel.

The man was walking sex: all tight olive skin over hard muscle. Tingling all over, she fought the desire to rip the towel off of him and lick every last droplet of water from that beautiful skin…and taste every inch of that hard body. "I'm curious by nature, my lord." *Especially about what's under that towel.* "I just want to know about the man I'm working for."

The corners of his mouth lifted slightly as he tracked her gaze. "If something interests you, then why do you not ask to see it?"

She didn't miss the double meaning. Her entire body tightened. Though she tried to keep her eyes on his face, deny his implication, it just wasn't possible to keep her eyes off his powerful body as he came toward her in his animal-like stride, the towel slipping with each step. She held her breath expectantly. Surely he did not mean to—

He stopped before her, took the ring from her fingers, and placed it in the box. She released the breath she had been holding and resisted the urge to inhale too deeply. He smelled clean, like musk and all things masculine.

"I will not have you going through my things. If I find anything missing, I will know instantly who to blame."

Her hand tingled from where their fingers had touched. What would those strong fingers feel like dancing over her neck and shoulders, stroking and plucking at her nipples, teasing— for doubtless he would tease her—with touches that inflamed without giving her the orgasm she sought…

The lid snapped shut—apparently he was satisfied she'd taken nothing. He turned back to her, his eyes now a darker blue. As he watched her intently, desire spread low into her belly. He lifted a dark brow, the cocky earl returning once more. "Well, since you seem to have nothing to do, and Jared is busy helping the cook with the inventory, you may help me with my clothes."

"Help with your clothes," she repeated, willing herself to concentrate as he moved away from her.

"I'll need riding attire," he threw over his shoulder.

Oh, well now that helped! Jeans and a T-shirt she understood, but riding clothes? What exactly did that mean?

He turned to the full-length mirror and began brushing his hair, offering her a great shot of his backside. The towel hung just below the indentations above his tight butt. His shoulders were broad, tapering down to a narrow waist and a firm butt made for squeezing. She'd bet her life she could bounce a quarter right off those high, taut cheeks.

He cleared his throat and her eyes shot back up to his reflection to find he watched her in the mirror, his expression indecipherable.

Pulling her thoughts out of the gutter, she focused on the task she'd been given and entered the closet that was larger than most bedrooms. There she found an extensive array of shirts, coats, pants, shoes, and boots, all arranged by color, starting with black and ending with white. Her lip curled in disbelief. What a clotheshorse! He was worse than any woman she knew.

"You will find a pair of buff-colored breeches and a linen shirt on the right side, above a pair of worn riding boots."

It took her less than a minute to find the exact pair of breeches—a remarkable feat in itself considering his clothes fetish. Anxious to leave his room and the sight of his nearly naked body, she laid the items out on the bed, picked up the bucket of now-cold, soapy water, and raced for the door when his voice stopped her.

"You're not finished yet."

"What now?" She cringed. She'd not meant to say the words out loud.

"Jared *always* helps me dress."

Her eyes narrowed, wondering if she'd heard him correctly. Certainly, he wasn't asking *her* to dress him, was he?

"I'm waiting," he said, his voice edged with impatience.

Taking a deep breath, she turned to face him. He stood with hands on hips in a stance so masculine she had a hard time remembering what he'd asked her. He raked a hand through his wet hair, the slight motion causing the muscles beneath his skin to bunch and flex. Though she'd never been the one-night-stand type, she couldn't help wondering what one night in his bed would be like. She bit her bottom lip…hard. She couldn't afford to be distracted by an infatuation that wouldn't end up going anywhere. After all, she would be leaving here as soon as she found the murderer.

She would not, under any circumstances, go to bed with him.

She straightened her shoulders and met his level gaze. Impossibly blue eyes stared back at her through long, thick lashes. She groaned inwardly. *Would a fling be so horrible? After all, you don't want a commitment—just mutual satisfaction. A fuck buddy, period.*

He had to know what his fantastic near-naked body was doing to her. He'd probably practiced that sensual stance in front of a mirror a thousand times. Steeling her resolve, she walked toward him. After all, how hard could it be to dress a grown man?

That question was answered a few seconds later as she stood on tiptoe and flung the shirt over his head, holding the sleeves open for his arms. For the love of God, she'd known children who were easier to dress! Frustrated, she quickly slipped the ends down over his bare torso, and stepped away only to see him frown.

"What?" Trying to keep the irritation out of her voice, she dropped her hands into fists at her sides.

"It's much too scratchy. Take it off." He watched her with lifted brow, obviously gauging her reaction.

You take it off! She wanted to yell, but she had no desire to start an argument. She wanted to get away, out of this room, and away from the sexual heat emanating from him. Instead she obediently yanked the shirt upwards, catching the opening around his neck, choking him. Amused, she pulled harder, and his arms got tangled up in the sleeves. The sound of tearing fabric rent the air, and abruptly the shirt gave way. She laughed under her breath, and he glared down at her.

She sobered instantly.

Throwing the shirt aside, he marched toward the wardrobe. Seconds later, he reappeared with a shirt on. Dropping the towel from around his waist, he snatched his pants off the bed, giving her a good—albeit brief—glimpse of his huge cock.

An uncomfortable warmth worked its way down to the very pit of her stomach, melting her insides.

At that exact moment Abigail, Christian's snooty cousin, walked through the door, her horrified aristocratic gaze shifting from Alex to Christian, who was busy jerking on his pants. She turned a lethal expression on Alex. "What are you doing in here?"

"She is doing her job," Christian said nonchalantly, buttoning his pants, evidently not bothered by how bad the situation looked. Sitting down he pulled on his boots. "Is it customary for you to walk into a room without knocking first?"

Abigail's cheeks turned bright red. "I thought—"

"If you and your brother still desire to go riding, please meet me at the stables in a quarter of an hour."

The dismissal in his tone couldn't be denied. Not even by Abigail, who left the room promptly, but only after throwing Alex a warning glare.

Christian stood, looking as debonair as ever, even when he wore what must be his most casual clothing. He passed by her, his masculine scent surrounding her. She yearned to take him down to the ground and have her way with him. She closed her eyes briefly, opening them when she heard him stop. "Alexandria," he said, his voice softer than she'd ever heard it.

She turned to find him within arm's reach, watching her intently. "Will you be serving dinner this evening?"

Her heart gave a little jolt. "Yes."

He reached out and brushed her jaw lightly. "I'm glad. Please be careful around Abigail." He winked. "She would have you horsewhipped if you 'ruined' another gown."

He ran the pad of his thumb along her lower lip. "Perhaps after dinner you can help me prepare for bed."

Alex watched him closely. The last had been almost an open invitation. His gaze shifted over her face, then he leaned into her, his lips lightly touching hers. She blinked stupidly and would have taken a step back had he not pulled her to him, crushing her breasts against his hard chest. Her tongue slipped past his lips and he smiled against her mouth, before deepened the kiss, his hands moving down her back and cupping her butt. He lifted her against his hard cock. Moaning, she wrapped her legs around his back and wove her fingers through his damp hair. His long fingers clenched her butt, pulling her tighter against his erection, sending a current of need straight to her slick folds. With a growl he walked a few steps until her back was up against the wall, his mouth hungry on hers. Excitement rippled along her spine. Never in all her years, had she experienced this kind of awareness.

He tore his mouth from hers, looking at her with dark, heavy-lidded eyes that promised her he would fuck her more than soundly. White-hot need raced through her body, to her breasts, her nipples ultra-sensitive. His gaze shifted to her lips, then to the pulse that beat heavily at her throat. The corners of his mouth lifted, and he bent his head, his lips touching her throat, there where her pulse raced madly, then lower over the swell of her breasts.

Her heart pounded so loud it was a roar in her ears. It took her a full minute to realize over the silken slide of Christian's talented tongue that it wasn't just the pounding of her heart, but the pounding of the door.

"My lord?"

Christian wrenched his mouth from hers, his eyes dark and full of passion. Alex unhooked her ankles and slid down his body.

"Just a moment, Jared." Christian's voice was husky. Alex took a step away from him, but before she could scurry away, he grabbed hold of her hand and pulled her back. A wicked smile on his lips, he kissed her soundly, lightly biting her bottom lip before releasing it. "I must play host now to my guests, but I look forward to this evening." He kissed her once more and patted her on the butt before striding toward the door.

Chapter Five

ာ

Alexandria shut the door to Devon's quarters behind her. "Now retrace your steps," she told Devon, who crossed the room and fell back on the bed with a contented sigh.

"I told you before. I came into the room, walked straight to the balcony where I drank my port and lit a cigar. I heard the door to my chamber open, and, assuming it was Jared, I told him I was out on the balcony. I heard the footsteps, then the next thing I knew, I was being pushed hard from behind."

"What do you remember of the killer? Were his hands big?"

"Alex, I don't remember. The impact knocked me off my feet, and up and over the railing."

Devon was right. It had to be a man.

"What about your journal? You mentioned you kept the names of all your acquaintances in there."

"Over in the top drawer," he said, motioning toward a mahogany dresser.

Time was of the essence. Christian would return from his ride shortly, and if Mimi or Jared found her, she'd be so busted. She rushed to the dresser and opened the drawer. Pushing aside stockings, she looked for the dark brown book with gold lettering Devon had described to her. "It's not here."

Devon frowned. "What do you mean it's not there?"

"I mean it's not here." She took the stockings out and showed him the empty drawer. "Where else could it be?"

"Maybe I left it in another drawer." Even he sounded unconvinced.

"Why would you hide a journal listing your friends and their addresses?"

"Well, as young men do, I used the journal not only to list my friends' addresses, but to mark which women I bedded."

Alex shook her head. Men had changed very little over the years. "How…unfortunate."

Devon frowned. "What do you mean, unfortunate?"

"You don't think that's a creepy thing to do?"

He shrugged. "A young man does not care what anyone thinks. It was customary for my university friends and I to place wagers on how many women we could get to our beds. Come, Alex, didn't you keep a list of your lovers?"

Alex snorted. "I didn't need a list. I only had one lover."

His brows lifted to his hairline. "One would think a lovely lass like you would have her pick of beaus."

She smiled at the compliment, and proceeded to check a nearby wardrobe for the journal.

"So…tell me, Alex, what happened to your lover?"

An unwanted image of Brad, her unfaithful fiancé, came to mind and just as quickly she willed it away. She had no desire to dig up her painful past. "He married my best friend, two weeks after he called off our wedding."

"And let me guess…you do not trust men now."

Could she keep nothing from him? "I don't think I ever trusted men. My father, loser that he was, rarely came through on a promise." She took a deep breath, shut the wardrobe door, and looked around the room. "Where else could we look?"

He scanned the room, his gaze fastening on the window and the landscape. "Looks like we need to get a move on. Christian is coming this way."

* * * * *

Christian's gaze shifted from the passing landscape to the windows of Devon's quarters. It was impossible not to remember the times when he'd come back from his morning ride to find Devon standing on his balcony, looking out over the lush fields or painting the landscape that he so loved. He would always wave exuberantly, a wide smile on his face. His brother had such a passion for life. Everyone who met Devon adored him. Christian could not think of a single enemy.

No wonder everyone thought he'd killed his older brother. It seemed he was the only one who had reason. If those accusers only knew how much he abhorred the aristocracy. Did they not wonder why he never ventured into London, save for business?

A flash passed one of the windows in his brother's quarters. Christian's heart gave a jolt. He pulled on his horse's reins and squinted. Did his eyes betray him? Then he saw it again. A shadow fell across one of the curtains. From this distance, he couldn't tell if it was man or woman, but clearly he could make out the outline of a figure moving within the room.

He glanced over his shoulder at Abigail and Reginald. "If you'll excuse me, I have to check on something."

Digging his heels into the horse's sides, he raced toward the manor, his heart pumping loudly in his ears. Everyone knew Devon's quarters were off-limits. Everyone. He had made it perfectly clear to everyone…including Alex. But what if the figure was Devon? Hope flared in his chest. Christian remembered the night he had clearly seen his brother. He'd been in his study, his head pounding as he went over the crop figures. Rain pelted against the windows, a draft had blown out a nearby candelabra. He had reached for a drink, and at that same moment saw Devon, standing before him. Christian had felt the blood leave his face, as he stood so suddenly the chair had fallen to the floor with a loud clatter. "Devon?" Christian had asked, and Devon smiled. A heartbeat later the door to the study had opened and Jared had popped his head in. "My lord, is everything all right? I thought I heard a noise."

"I am fine." When he turned back, Devon had disappeared and Christian had not seen him since. He had not shared that experience with anyone. In fact, he'd convinced himself that his overtaxed mind had conjured up his brother's image because he'd missed him so desperately.

No, it probably was not Devon wandering about his quarters, but rather a curious servant.

*Alexandria again…*He jumped from his horse and took the stairs two at a time. Fury filled every inch of him. How dare Alexandria go in Devon's chambers! Particularly when he had specifically told her not to.

He raced past shocked maids who scrambled to get out of his way. Throwing open the door to Devon's quarters, he stopped abruptly, noticing immediately the musty smell of the closed up room. His gaze darted around, looking for any sign of the intruder. "I know you are here, so you may as well show yourself."

Seconds passed, and still no one stepped from behind the sheet-draped furniture or the velvet curtains. Nothing seemed out of sorts—save that the door of the balcony appeared to be ajar. Crossing the room in long strides, he ripped open the double doors, only to find the balcony empty.

His brows furrowed into a frown as he stepped out. Grabbing onto the rail for support, he looked over the side, but saw no one. He ran a hand through his hair. Perhaps his mind was playing tricks on him after all.

That thought disappeared a second later when he heard a rustle of brush beneath him.

* * * * *

Alex's heart hammered against her ribs. That had been way too close! She should have known Christian would return before she could thoroughly search Devon's quarters.

Brushing the dirt from her gown, she hastily tidied the hair that had fallen out of her sloppy bun while climbing down the trellis beside Devon's third floor bedchamber. Thank God Christian had the decorative iron fencing yanked out after

Devon's fall, or she might have suffered a similar fate. In her younger years, she had sneaked out of her second story window to meet up with friends, but she had managed it in jeans and sweatshirts. It was an entirely different experience hanging from three stories above, wearing a long dress that had absolutely no give to the fabric.

Trying to regain a normal pulse, she walked toward the back door in what she hoped appeared to be a leisurely pace. Alex flinched when the door swung open.

"Alex, where have you been?" Mimi asked from the doorway. "His lordship is looking for you."

"He is? I've been out here…cutting blossoms for the dinner table," she said, despite the fact she stood empty-handed. Spying a basket on a nearby bench, she quickly snatched it up. "I was just coming back to get this."

Mimi had the grace not to call her a liar, though her skeptical expression said as much. "Well, the flowers will have to wait. His lordship's summons was most urgent."

"Indeed," Christian said, stepping out from behind Mimi. Alex's stomach dropped to her toes. He didn't look happy.

"That will be all, Mimi. Thank you." As he walked toward Alex in long strides, his gaze never wavered. He didn't so much as blink.

The empty basket felt strangely heavy in Alex's hand. Who was she trying to fool? He knew she had been in Devon's room. She could see the condemnation in his eyes. It would be much simpler if she could just tell him the truth—that she'd traveled through time to help him, but that was even more complicated than trying to explain why she'd been in Devon's room.

"You were looking for me, my lord?" Her voice sounded strangled even to her own ears.

The smile on Christian's lips didn't even come close to reaching his eyes. "Someone was in Devon's quarters. It would be an unfair assumption to say I believed it was you who were the guilty party, particularly after our recent conversation on the matter. Yet I find it odd that you are out here, with an empty basket, and your cheeks flushed from exertion. Not to mention your hair and clothes are disheveled." He took a step closer to her and plucked a leaf from her hair. "Either you were in Devon's room…or you were out cavorting with a lover."

Alex could feel the heat in her cheeks increase as he stared at her accusingly. It was hard to believe that just hours before she'd been in his arms, kissing him…wrapping her legs around his waist. Now he watched her with indifference. If she admitted to being in Devon's room, he would never trust her…and that wouldn't do.

"I was with a man." At least it wasn't a lie. She had been with Devon.

"Who?" he asked, his voice gruff.

"I prefer not to say."

He lifted a dark brow. "Does he work in this household?"

Dear God, she was just getting herself in deeper with every minute. She shook her head. "No."

His brows furrowed into a frown. "Yet you were just with him? How is it that you have been at Radborne Manor for only a few days and have managed to find a lover…one who does not even work for me?"

Her cheeks blazed hot under his skeptical glare. "Who said he was my lover? We are friends, that's all."

It was like a thundercloud had rolled in overhead. His jaw clenched tight, a nerve ticking there. The fury inside him built with every second. Why was he so mad? It's not as if he had a claim to her…

Alex groaned inwardly. Why hadn't she just told him the truth? It would have been easier to defend herself than to make up some fantasy boyfriend that would only cause more trouble for her. "I wasn't in Devon's quarters," she said, hoping to divert his attention. "I'm sorry you thought it was me."

His expression turned quickly from rage to what appeared to be irritation. "Miss Drake, you and your *friend* must remember not to meet on my time."

"Yes, my lord," she replied, noticing he was back to addressing her formally. Unable to meet his gaze, her gaze shifted to his cravat.

"Very well, that is all."

She nodded and left him, feeling his eyes burning into her every step down the walkway.

* * * * *

She had a lover? No, a *male friend*, and yet if they were only friends, then why, pray tell, would she have leaves in her hair? He had no idea, which irritated him more; the thought she had a lover…or that she had gone against his demands to stay out of Devon's quarters.

Alexandria was a sexual woman. He had evidence of that this morning in his chambers. True, he had started things with a kiss, but she had quickly wound her long legs around his waist and locked her ankles, her moans telling him that she had experienced the act before. Her practiced kisses, the way she moved against his erection, squirming, like she needed to take every inch of him within her tight, firm body…He released an unsteady breath. She would be a vixen in bed, a woman that could easily bring a man to his knees.

As he watched her walk into the manor, his gut tightened. Why was she so interested in Devon? And why had she gone through Christian's own desk, and his jewelry box? Who was Alexandria Drake? His thoughts took an abrupt turn and shifted to the men in his employ, the majority who were in their twentieth year and some closer to their thirtieth. Which of those men was Alex's *friend*? She had said the man was not in his employ, but could he believe her…or was she lying about that too?

To his dismay, the questions regarding Alex burned within him throughout the long day, and he even found himself looking forward to dinner when he would see her again.

And just when he had sat down with a much-needed drink, Alex's laughter reached out to him. He glanced out the window and saw her with Mimi. The two were walking across the lawns, toward the stables where Mimi's brother worked. Perhaps her lover was Michael, the stable master. An attractive man in his mid-twenties, Michael had caught the favor of many of Radborne's maids.

A vision of Alex's long legs wrapped around the younger man's waist, looking at the younger man with the same heavy-lidded look she had given Christian just this morning came unheeded and he swore under his breath.

Alex smiled up at the younger man and laughed at something he said.

Christian put a hand up to the cool window. "Who are you, Alexandria?" he asked again. A cool draft surrounded him, and in the window he caught a reflection beside his own. His heart skipped a beat recognizing the familiar face. "Devon?"

He turned abruptly, only to find himself alone. To his horror, Reginald appeared out of the shadows, his brows lifted in question. "Did you say something, Strathmore?"

God, he hoped his cousin had not heard him speak his brother's name. "No, nothing."

Reginald's lips quirked. "Right. Well...I did not mean to interrupt you. I merely wanted to thank you for the delightful ride this morning, but I see you are busy, so I shall see you at supper this evening." With a curt nod, he left Christian alone.

Christian fell into a chair and ran his fingers through his hair. Had it been Reginald? The man had a creepy knack for showing up at the oddest times and in the oddest places. Perhaps it *had* been Devon...

What was he thinking? Lord help him...he was losing his mind. The last thing he needed was a distant cousin spreading word that the current Earl of Strathmore had gone mad.

Chapter Six

ဆာ

When Alex got back to the twentieth century, she was going to get her own maid: someone to cook, clean, and scour her house. Never again would she lift a finger. Throwing dust rag over a bust of Charles II, she dropped onto a settee to survey her handy work. She put her hands behind her head and breathed a heavy sigh. She had been in this century for a little under a week and couldn't get adjusted to the schedule. Even when she was supposed to be off of work, she still worked. It seemed Christian called her for every little thing. *Alex, get me some tea. Alex, come tell me, is the white shirt more to your liking, or the dark?* Why in the hell didn't he just ask his cousin? She would leap at the chance to help him.

But it appeared he had no interest in his cousin. In fact, he always looked pained when in her presence, always excusing himself, but not before offering the use of his carriage or horses.

The clock on the wall struck two, the bell tolling twice, reminding Alex that she didn't have time to dawdle. Within quarter of an hour she would be expected in the kitchen to help with dinner.

Why had she told Christian she came to the manor looking for work? She should have said she had amnesia, or was the daughter of a rich monarch of a remote country that didn't exist. At least then she could have kicked back and been a guest, rather than a slave.

And more importantly, she would have more time to spend on Devon's case. The case was perplexing. How in the world had someone pulled off a murder in a house full of over two hundred people? There had been no witnesses, and now even Devon's journal had come up missing.

While working in the kitchen, Alex tried to get any information about the night of the murder from the other servants. Every last person she asked seemed appalled she had brought up the former earl. One maid though had mentioned his bounty of mistresses. She had lifted her brows in a way that invited speculation, and then muttered something about Christian putting his brother to shame with his legion of lovers.

No doubt Christian's virility was legendary. How could it not be? She'd seen his cock for herself, and had felt it. She shifted, remembering the hard ridge of flesh against her slick entrance. If only their clothing had not been between them. She squeezed her thighs together, recalling the sensations, the raw need.

Male voices sounded on the other side of the library door. Before Alex could stand up, Christian stepped into the room, followed by Reginald, who shut the door behind him.

Alex dropped onto the rug, and on hands and knees, crawled behind the settee to wait for the two men to leave. Damn! Alex moaned inwardly, knowing that she had left the rag over the bust of Charles II. Surely one of the men would see it and comment.

The sound of liquid splashing into a cup broke the silence. "May I offer you a drink?" Christian asked.

Moments later Christian sat on the settee Alex had just occupied.

"Thank you," Reginald replied. "I am delighted you sought me out before the evening meal. We have had little time to get to know one another, and I hope to remedy that."

Reginald cleared his throat. "I am also glad we had this moment to talk without my sister being privy to our conversation."

"Oh, and why is that?"

"You know women. They want to speak of frivolous things, such as the latest styles and the weather, while I am more interested in learning about…well, you for instance." Reginald laughed, an annoying feminine chuckle that made Alex cringe. "I am wondering if you have heard any news on Devon's murder?"

Alex frowned. Why would Reginald bring up such a forbidden subject?

She could hear Christian shift in the settee. "Detective Thacker is calling it an accident."

"Ah, I see. And are you of the same opinion?"

"I believe my brother was pushed to his death. He would not have slipped over the rail by accident."

"Perhaps he was well into his cups?"

"My brother rarely drank." The words were clipped and curt.

"Oh dear, I see I have angered you. Please forgive me." The man's voice lacked conviction.

"Tell me, Reginald. How long will you and your sister be visiting?"

Reginald coughed and an uncomfortable silence followed. "I…I do not know."

"As you are aware, things have been difficult for me since my brother's sudden passing. I find myself occupied with business matters and I do not feel I am an adequate host at this time. Perhaps you would enjoy staying at my London townhouse? There would be more for you and Abigail to do, and I am certain in the city you would find company more to your liking."

"Perhaps I can be of assistance to you? I have experience in handling estates—"

"Thank you, but no." Christian's tone was matter-of-fact. "I prefer to handle it on my own."

"I will broach the subject with Abigail this evening. I would not want to stay where we are not wanted…"

Alex held her breath, hoping Christian didn't rise to the bait.

Christian set the glass down on the table and stood. If he turned just a hair to the right, he could easily see her crouched behind the settee. She didn't dare move a fraction. He would be so furious with her if he caught her spying. "As much as I hate to cut our conversation short, there are a few things I need to attend to before dinner."

"Very well."

She heard them walk toward the door then it opened and closed.

Alex peeked around the corner of the settee to find Christian watching her, his arms crossed over his chest. "Good afternoon, Alexandria."

With a sigh, she stood. "How did you know I was in here?"

"For one, you left your rag over my mother's prized bust of Charles II. For another, I saw you when we entered—lounging on the settee."

He crossed the room toward her, stopping only to pick the rag off Charles II. "Never have I met a maid with such an aversion to work."

Alex smiled despite her effort not to. "I have to confess that I don't particularly like housework. In fact, maybe there's a position in the kitchen? I like to cook, and I'm quite good at it."

He brushed a wayward strand of hair over her ear. "Is that so?"

His touch did strange things to her. She liked it…a lot. Despite all the drama since her arrival, the fact of the matter was she wanted him. Not in a schoolgirl crush sort of way, but in a have-to-have-him-or-I-won't-be-able-to-stand-it kind of way. Her gaze wandered over his chiseled features, the dark blue eyes that watched her so warily now. How tumultuous their relationship had been from the word go. She didn't want him angry with her. No, she wanted his hands on her body, wanted him kissing her with the raw ferocity she'd experienced before in his arms. "Yes."

His lips quirked. "Well, then perhaps I should have a talk with Georgette, the cook—see if she could use the help. I have a feeling she will not decline, but I must warn you, she is a stern taskmaster. There will be no lollygagging about."

Alex nodded. "Thank you. You won't regret this decision. I swear."

His eyes softened as he watched her, taking on that heavy-lidded look that made her pulse quicken and her stomach tighten. A look that said, *I want you, and I'll stop at nothing to have you.*

"Why is it that I can not stay mad at you, Alex? You anger me like no other, yet with a flash of your smile, I find myself…"

He leaned forward and kissed her hard, his tongue teasing against her lips, before stroking hers. He tasted of fine brandy, smooth and sweet. Her arms encircled his neck, and he smiled against her lips.

His long hair brushed against her fingers, and she couldn't help but run her fingers through the silky strands.

"You make me mad with desire," he whispered against her lips, catching her bottom lip with his teeth, sucking lightly, before letting loose and kissing her once more.

His hand moved to her breast, his fingers teasing her already-hard nipples. She wanted to feel his lips there, teasing her, his teeth gently biting as he'd done to her bottom lip mere seconds before.

The door opened abruptly, the squeak of the hinges alerting them. Alex jumped away from Christian, who turned to the door, a frown on his face.

It was Reginald. "Forgive me, I did not mean to interrupt. I had a question, but it can wait." He looked from Christian to Alex.

Reginald's dark brown eyes assessed her as one would an insect, slowing at her breasts. No doubt he could see her erect nipples, her swollen lips, Christian's ruffled hair. Resisting the urge to crawl behind Christian, Alex instead met his dark gaze without blinking.

He returned his attention to Christian. "I shall see you at dinner." He bowed and backed out of the room, shutting the door firmly behind him.

Alex winced. "Great, that's just what you needed."

Christian shrugged. "He is a houseguest, and a cousin twice removed. I met him for the first time a month before Devon's passing. I know nothing about him, save for the fact he enjoys drinking from the collection of Madeira I brought back from Portugal five years ago. A collection that is fast diminishing."

"He seemed disappointed in you just then."

"I think he envies me." Christian took the step that separated them and kissed her lightly. His hand wandered up to her breast, and his long fingers rolled over her nipple in a way that sent a shockwave straight to her already-slick folds. The heated look in his blue eyes told her knew exactly what she was thinking.

She put a hand on his chest and felt his heart leap beneath her fingers. "I don't think that was envy. I think he's furious, especially since he's trying to set you up with his sister."

Christian's throat convulsed, and Alex smiled inwardly. "I have no interest in Abigail."

Yes! "Why are they here then?"

"I know Devon met them last year while taking holiday in Paris. No doubt he invited them to visit. I find I am not the host my brother was. He enjoyed parties, loved having friends over. I prefer solitude to parties and the crush of the aristocracy." Her fingers brushed over his flat nipple. He stiffened. "Be careful, Alex."

"Careful of what, Christian?" She kept her voice low, seductive.

He lowered his head, kissing her.

A loud crash sounded from a nearby room and Christian groaned against her lips. "I cannot wait until those two leave this house."

"How do you know it was one of them?"

"Because if it were a servant Jared would be bellowing right about now. No doubt he will be coming this way, so you had best get back to work." He lifted her hand to his lips and kissed her fingers. "I will talk to cook this afternoon."

"Thank you."

His gaze wandered over her, his features strained. He wanted her. Her heart soared. She smiled, and shut the door behind her.

* * * * *

Christian steadied himself against the balustrade. He had drunk far too much tonight. Tripping on the final step, he landed face down on the floor. He shook his head. Reginald, who was snoring on the settee in the library, might have had the right idea.

Pushing himself to his feet, Christian ran his hand along the wall to feel his way down the dark hallway. He stopped in front of Alex's door. His heart pounded erratically, imagining Alex in bed, wearing nothing, her soft curves illuminated by the moonlight. He had no business being here, and well he knew it. Yet, all evening his gaze had been drawn to her. When serving him she had brushed up against him, her scent enveloping him, luring him in. It had been difficult to focus on the conversation going on around him. Reginald's intense stare did not help either. His cousin watched Alex, his lascivious gaze fastened on her as he called her over to replenish his glass time and again.

To Alex's credit she had served Reginald, a practiced smile on her lips, ignoring the bold glances he cast her way.

"Don't do it," he said under his breath, even as he turned the knob and entered her room. He shouldn't be here. Yet he could not stay away.

He closed the door behind him.

Shadows played against the walls as the light from the candle on the nightstand illuminated the bed where Alex lay on her back, one hand resting on her stomach, the other thrown over her head. Her hair fell across her white pillow like a reddish-gold cloud, beckoning him to feel the soft texture. The black of her lashes lay against the delicate cream color of her skin, and her lips were slightly parted. He smiled. She looked so innocent.

Looks could be deceiving.

Before he could stop himself, he fell into a nearby chair and stared at the woman who had found her way into his dreams of late...and was fast making her way into his heart. He yearned for her touch. He yearned for an end to this attraction that was taking over his every waking thought. Tonight when he had kissed her in the library, she had returned his kiss fiercely, her moans telling him that she wanted him as desperately as he wanted her. And then the way her fingers had stroked his nipple while she looked at him so brazenly...and then pulled his nipple teasingly. Had Reginald not interrupted them, he could have taken her right there on the library floor and she would have allowed it...welcomed it.

His cock strained against the fabric of his pants.

"Christian?"

Startled out of his thoughts, he blinked to find the object of his desire propped up on an elbow watching him, a frown marring her beautiful features.

"I shouldn't have come," he said, making a move to stand from the chair.

She sat up, the slight motion sent the sheet to her lap, and to his chagrin he could not look away from the sight of her rosy nipples pressed against the thin material of her chemise. "I want you to stay."

Sitting back down, he nearly toppled over in the chair. He was too drunk and he didn't want to fall asleep in her room. Then he'd have a lot to explain. "I did not mean to wake you."

Alex's heart constricted seeing Christian sitting in the chair, his slightly mussed hair and reddened eyes telling her he had more than a few drinks. "I think you know why you came," she offered, throwing the blankets from her.

His gaze shifted to her breasts and he smiled—a boyish smile that stole her breath away.

He blinked several times before focusing once again on her face. "You amaze me, Alexandria Drake. You do exactly what you want, uncaring of what others think of you." His smile faded abruptly and he opened his mouth to say something then quickly closed it. A second later, he ran trembling hands down his face. "I really should not be here."

"But you *are* here."

When he made the slightest move to stand, she was off the bed, pushing him back down. With a wicked smile, she straddled his hips. He blinked a few times as though he couldn't believe she now sat astride him. She smelled the brandy on his breath, saw the vulnerability in his eyes, and felt the thick, hard erection against her sensitive core. Placing a hand on either side of his face, she leaned forward and touched her lips to his. It started as a sweet kiss, tentative, but it instantly took on a heated intensity.

Deepening the kiss, needing him with a ferocity that had been denied for too long, she looped her arms around his neck. She opened her mouth, sliding her tongue against his, tasting him, stroking it in a familiar rhythm. His hands moved down her back, cupping her ass, pulling her heated flesh against his throbbing cock.

She groaned low in her throat as their mouths met again—parrying, dipping, and plunging. His cocked twitched against her belly, and the blood in her veins heated, swooping lower to her already-damp folds.

The sweet brandy on his tongue, the pungent sandalwood mingled with his own masculine scent, drove her desire to a higher level. She needed his hands on her body, touching her, taking her to that place she'd been yearning for since the moment she'd met him. Her hands moved over his hard chest and hard stomach, ripping the shirt out of his pants so she could feel his flesh beneath her fingertips.

His lips left hers to run a slow path from her jaw, to her ear, his teeth nipping her lobe, before moving down her neck. His warm lips stopped at the pulse beating wildly, kissed her there before proceeding further, to the swell of her breasts. He lifted the chemise from her and tossed it aside.

Her heart gave a little jolt. Tonight there would be no interruptions. Tonight they would finish what they had started. Exultation washed over her and she buried her hands in his hair. He smiled against her breast before his tongue circled her nipple, hot, wet, velvety soft, sucking hard…

She moaned as he grazed his teeth over the sensitive peak, driving her crazy with need. His hands on her hips clenched tight, moving her up and down the length of his rock-hard cock. The blood heated in her veins, spreading throughout her body.

Alex's hands worked the buttons of his pants and unleashed his cock. She touched the velvety softness of his throbbing shaft. Her breath left her in a rush. It had been too long since she'd felt the power of a cock in her hand. The delicious feel of satin over steel. She stroked him from the plum-size head to the thick base.

His head fell back against his shoulders, his mouth slightly open, his eyes half-mast. She loved the power, had forgotten the satisfaction of making a man wild with need with a simple caress. Heat swooped low in her belly, sending a tremor of need straight between her legs.

She stood, long enough to pull his pants down over his hips, and off. While he complied, he watched her intently, his eyes dark with passion, promising her with a heated stare that they had only just begun. "You are well aware that we are passing the point of no return?"

Humored by his concern of her virtue, she glanced at his rock-hard cock that swelled past his belly button. "I'm aware." His cock twitched and her gaze returned to his face. "Are you having second thoughts?"

His gaze moved down over her body, stopping at her breasts, over the gentle swell of her stomach and then lower still. Excitement raced along her spine as his eyes returned to hers. He shook his head. "Alex, come here."

Climbing back on his lap, she sank down on his erection, her breath leaving her in a rush as he stretched her honeyed walls.

His hands moved to her waist, holding her, making her take it slow as they both watched his cock disappear inside of her. Her body tightened around him, pulling him in further, until she had taken it all. She didn't move, savoring the feel, the wonderful ache.

With a groan, Christian kissed a breast, his tongue circling the nipple. He rolled the other nipple between finger and thumb.

The combination of his mouth on her breasts and his cock inside of her brought Alex instantly to orgasm. Her breathing increased as she rode out the white-hot need inside her. Rotating her hips, she moaned low in her throat at the delicious sensations. "That was fast," she said, and the cocky grin on his face mirrored the way she felt.

Abruptly he stood, without saying a word but still grinning, his hands clasping her bottom as he walked them unsteadily over to the bed. He kissed her, following her down onto the mattress.

He towered over her, just the head of his cock inside her now. She spread her legs wider and lifted her hips to take more of him in. He moved the tip in and out of her until she writhed beneath him, her groin stirring, need tightening her belly. "Christian, please…"

He plunged into her, touching her womb, his face strained. His eyes closed as he filled her. Inside her, Christian's cock grew thicker and longer, stretching her. God she had missed this, the feeling of a man inside her, taking her to the stars.

Leaning over her, he kissed her hard. "You were made for loving, Alex."

He began to move, his hips thrusting in slow, controlled strokes. She watched his body join hers, saw his eyes darken and then he looked at her. The heat in his eyes made her pulse skitter. His hands moved to her breasts, taking them in his hands, his fingers playing with her nipples until they were diamond hard. Once again, her blood quickened in her veins, sending shockwaves of desire throughout her body. With each thrust the white-hot need heightened, building in her until…

Like waves slamming against the shore, she came, her sheath clutched his cock, throbbing, pulling him in deeper. Alex cried out in ecstasy, riding the wave of the best orgasm of her life.

She opened her eyes and found him watching her, a devilish grin on his face. A grin that disappeared a moment later as he lifted her ass and thrust within her. The veins in his neck were pronounced as he increased his strokes, setting off another orgasm, even grander than the first.

He came with a groan, his heart pounding hard against her own. They stayed like that, their limbs entwined, until she could hear his even breathing. She smiled inwardly. He had fallen asleep in her room. Perhaps she should wake him just in case Jared discovered where his master had fallen asleep? She looked over at Christian, the harsh planes of his face softened in sleep.

There might be hell to pay tomorrow…but she would let him sleep.

Chapter Seven

ඞ

Christian opened an eye and was immediately sorry when the pressure in his head threatened to explode. Sunlight streamed through the windows, causing him to throw the sheet over his head and beg for tomorrow to come.

"Now you see what overindulgence does."

Groaning out loud, he waited for Jared's speech on the sins of alcohol. But that was forgotten as the smell of eggs assailed Christian's nostrils, sending his stomach curling to his throat. "Take that plate away, or you will find yourself out of a job."

"You could never replace me, my lord, and you well know it," came the steady reply, before the scrape of the dish against the tray could be heard. The sound of the door being closed louder than necessary followed his departure…and it was at that moment Christian realized where he was.

Alexandria's room.

Looking down at the sheets wrapped around his naked body, he remembered bits and pieces of the night past. After dinner he and Reginald had played a friendly game of chess. His cousin had constantly refilled his glass while they talked of business, weather, and his sister. Reginald had passed out on the parlor settee.

As the minutes passed and the fog of drink-induced dreams subsided, reality became painfully clear as he remembered kissing Alex, and then the feel of her sweet body…

Pulling himself up out of bed, he quickly donned his clothes that were scattered about the room. Opening the door, he looked down the dark hallway and made a hasty retreat to his quarters.

As luck would have it, Reginald was coming up the stairs from the parlor as Christian was coming down the servants' wing. "Christian, I would wish you good morning, but I can see by the pallor of your skin you are of the same mind as I. I want only to find my bed and sleep the day away."

"As do I," Christian said, stopping on the stair above his cousin.

"Where did you pass the night?"

Christian groaned inwardly. He was leaving the servants' quarters after a night of heavy drinking. It did not take a genius to figure out where he'd been. "In the hallway of all places. You are well and truly foxed when you get lost in your own house." Without saying another word, he nodded, and continued down the stairs.

Thankfully Jared had seen to the bath. Steam rolled off the water, inviting him to step in and draw the ache from his sore body. Undressing, Christian sank down into the bath, wishing the water could soak out all the alcohol in his body. If only it were that easy.

Twenty minutes later, he had fallen into a hazy slumber with his head rolled back on the edge of the tub, when his conscience came through the door and stood before him.

"You owe Miss Drake an apology, my lord. Not only did you manage to make a spectacle of yourself by sneaking into her quarters at night, but by your lack of dress this morning, I must assume the worst. Let us hope she does not end up with child."

Memories of the night before flooded him. Alex's cries of surrender, the way her hands had latched onto his ass, craving every inch of his cock. They had made love several times throughout the night, her soft groans urging him on. Unless Alex kept French Letters in her dresser drawer, they had not used protection, and he could not recall if he had withdrawn in time. Any other time the thought of being a father would startle him. Yet he imagined for a moment a baby girl with auburn curls and green eyes, like her mother's.

"My lord, I am only looking out for your well-being."

Christian knew Jared was sincere. He only had his best interests at heart.

Jared had the grace not to say another word. With a regal bow, he walked out the door.

An hour later Christian had made it downstairs with no problems, glad to get to the dining room before Abigail or Reginald made an appearance. Perhaps he could finish his meal before they made it down. He was in no mood for polite conversation. What had happened to the days when he could handle his liquor? He couldn't recall ever feeling as rotten as he did now.

He reached for the newspaper when the kitchen door opened and Alex walked in. She set the cup before him, her arm brushing against his as she leaned forward and poured the coffee. "Good morning, my lord."

Her silky soft voice made the hair on his arms stand on end. He remembered her sweet moans last night as he'd filled her, the way her long legs had hooked around his back, the way her honeyed walls had felt…

His cock stirred to life again.

She looked at him, her green eyes soft, warm, inviting. "How do you feel?"

Aroused is how he felt. He grabbed her free hand, running his thumb over the rapid pulse in her wrist. He was not the only one affected. "Better now."

She smiled and to his astonishment his heart missed a beat. "I'm glad."

Voices out in the hallway alerted him to his cousins' presence. He dropped Alex's hand a moment before the dining room door opened and Reginald and Abigail walked in.

Alex hurried to the kitchen.

"I thought you were sleeping the day away." Christian tried to keep the disappointment out of his voice, but failed.

Reginald shook his head. "I wanted to, but Abigail insisted I wake. Plus, a few hours did wonders. By the way, thought you'd leave me laying on the settee, huh?" he said, clapping Christian on the back as though they were lifelong friends and not virtual strangers.

"I was not about to toss you over my shoulder and take you to your room."

"Not likely when you were as foxed as I," Reginald said, flashing a grin.

Further conversation was cut short as Alex walked through the door with plates filled with eggs, ham, and sweetbread.

"What a lovely day it is, my lord. I was wondering if you would be interested in showing me the rest of Radborne's vast lands today." Abigail's voice cut into his thoughts.

Alex did not once look at Christian, but instead focused solely on her task. Abigail lifted her chin a good inch and watched Alex closely while she set a plate down.

Abigail was what he hated about the aristocracy. The aura of being superior to everyone, save one's peers. "I have business to attend to, but I'm sure your brother has time to ride with you."

Alex's lips curved in a small smile. Apparently she liked his answer.

Reginald nodded. "Indeed, I do have time. I would be delighted to show you what our cousin cannot."

Alex rounded the table and set Christian's plate before him. How tempted he was to pull her onto his lap, to kiss her before these two who would be horrified that he dallied with a servant.

Desperate to be away from the two, Christian ate his breakfast in record time, and left his cousins to finish. He wished they would just leave him alone. Go back to Paris, or even take his advice and visit his London townhouse. Lord knows he wouldn't be needing it anytime soon. He could not understand why anyone would want to burden their family members by arriving out of nowhere, when they were never invited to stay to begin with. Very strange.

He retired to his study, wanting and needing solace. Sitting in his chair, he ran his hands through his hair, trying to focus on estate business he should attend to. For all that he tried to concentrate, his thoughts turned back to the night before. Alex had been a wonderful lover. Her soft sighs had spurred him on, begging him to take her higher and further. His blood stirred recalling the way she'd yanked his pants off him, her devilish smile as she'd straddled him, the heavy-lidded look in her haunting eyes as she'd taken him into her body. She'd been so responsive to his lovemaking, unafraid to say what she wanted and do what she wanted. He had never had such an uninhibited lover.

The door opened and the woman who'd been burning in his thoughts appeared. Closing the door behind her, she leaned back against the door and smiled. "I was hoping you'd retire to your study."

"Come here," he said, standing and moving toward her. She pushed away from the door and met him halfway, throwing her arms around his neck. With a groan, he kissed her, drawing her tongue into his mouth, sucking it, before parrying it with his own. Her hand slid over his erection with a practiced caress. The blood burned in his veins, sending a throbbing need to his cock.

She smiled against his lips. "You're already hard?"

He pulled away for a moment. "I've been thinking of you…about last night." Recalling the feel of her slick folds beneath his fingers, his hand slipped between her legs, stroking her through the fabric of her skirt, but it wasn't enough. He lifted the skirt and found her naked beneath. With a groan, he unbuttoned his pants, pushed them down, and turned Alex around. She braced her arms against the solid mahogany desk her back arched, her ass high.

He ran his fingers over her dewy cleft, and then with a single thrust, filled her to the womb. Her breath left her in a rush. His hands on her hips, he thrust slowly, his cock impossibly hard and she took every inch inside her hot, wet channel. She reached back, grabbing his ass, encouraging him with her soft whimpers moving her hips against him, urging him deeper, harder, faster.

"Mary, please see that there are fresh flowers placed in our guests' rooms." Jared's voice penetrated the wall, alerting them. Alex's head jerked up, her hand falling away from his ass. She moved to pull away, but he held her hips fast.

She glanced at the closed door, pausing, waiting.

He moved slowly, withdrawing, the tip of his cock at her entrance. She bit into her bottom lip and he smiled.

The voices carried further down the hall, and he entered her. Her hand returned to his ass, squeezing, encouraging him.

He tightened his grip on her hips, nearly lifting her off her feet with each down-stroke. She cried out, her vagina pulsing, pulling him in deeper, milking him, his body throbbing with pleasure. Her heavenly sighs took him over the edge and he came with a growl.

Alex pulled her skirt down and turned to him with a smile. "I had better get back to the kitchen before they notice I've been gone too long." She moved to the door but he stopped her, drawing her into his arms.

"I do regret that I was so horrible to you. As you know it is a difficult time for me, and I did not mean to take out my frustrations on you."

Her face softened and she went up on her toes and kissed him. "I forgive you."

He patted her on her high, firm ass. "Yes, it is best you go…because if you stay here, you will distract me and I will not get this business finished."

She reached out, ran her hand over his cock and smiled sweetly. "See you later."

Chapter Eight

෨

Later that evening Alexandria paused on the landing, looking down over the banister to see if anyone was around. Certain that all the other servants were busy eating their meal, she slipped into Jared's room. Her hand trembled as she shut the door behind her.

Devon might think Jared wouldn't hurt either him or Christian, but Alex needed to be certain.

She pulled open the top drawer of his dresser and did a quick check for Devon's journal. Her heart pounded as her fingers grazed what felt like a book. When she lifted it from the drawer, a combination of relief and disappointment swept through her at finding a volume of poetry by Byron.

Finding nothing out of the ordinary, she went onto the next room. One by one, she checked each servant's drawers, working quickly for fear of getting caught.

Entering Mimi's room, Alex experienced a brief pang of guilt. In her short time here, she'd come to care for the other woman.

Hearing footsteps coming her way, Alex stopped and held her breath. How could she explain her presence in Mimi's room, and would anyone buy it? What trust she had gained would be erased, and she could even lose her job. God, what then?

She released the breath a moment later when the person passed by. Knowing she had to get back downstairs or risk getting caught, Alex searched the room. She found nothing for her effort. She had a hand on the knob when she caught a glimpse of a book sticking out the slightest bit from under Mimi's pillow.

Alex's pulse skittered. Surely it wasn't Mimi who had taken the journal. Why would Mimi have it? She crossed the room and reached for the book.

She knew what she held the moment she saw the brown leather book with the gold-lettered initials DJR. Her stomach clenched in a tight knot.

Devon's journal.

She opened the journal, skimmed over the pages of elegant writing. There were a lot of names here, a lot of information to look over. If she took it, surely Mimi would realize it right away. In a quandary, Alex decided she had to take the journal back to her room, read it tonight, and replace it first thing tomorrow. If Mimi came knocking on her door tonight, well—she'd just have to deal with it. Exiting the room as quietly as she'd entered, Alex went directly to her room and hid the journal in her top drawer.

Her mind raced as she shut the door behind her and hurried down to the next floor. Why would Mimi want Devon dead? It was obvious the girl had cared for Devon, perhaps even loved him. What would have made her want him dead then? Mimi had mentioned that Abigail had arrived at the party and had actively pursued him. Had Mimi and Devon had a sexual relationship? Was it jealousy that drove her to push him over the balcony?

But history didn't lie, and whoever killed Devon, would also kill Christian. Unless she could stop it. Mimi had lived at Radborne manor all her life. Why would she risk it? It didn't make sense. Yet if Mimi were the suspect, Christian was in even more danger than Devon had anticipated. Living under the same roof as the person you planned to murder offered limitless opportunity.

Passing by Christian's room, an image of how he'd looked last night when he'd come to her room flashed before her. Although Christian was drunk at the time, he'd come to her, and he'd made love to her all night long. It had been wonderful to wake up with his strong arms around her, holding her tight, like he never wanted to let her go. When she had gone to him in the study she had no intention of making love to him again, but she was thrilled to find that the night before had not been a drunken mistake on his part. He had made her body sing with his skilled touch, making her feel like she could soar to the stars.

Could she get enough of him? What if she failed in her mission? Her heart gave a hard jerk. She could not fail. This man already had worked his way into her soul. Already she could not wait until tonight.

He'd told her to come to him, via the servants' staircase. Apparently there was a secret stairwell that would take her straight to his room. She cringed recalling the staircase Christian had dragged her down her first day at Radborne Manor. She would have to bring a candle to light her way, but the claustrophobia would be worth it, because Christian would be waiting for her.

She couldn't wait to finish with her chores. She would take a bath in rosewater, wear her hair up, and put on a chemise. No, a robe. She wished she had a silk robe, or something that formed to her body instead of the bulky robe all servants were given. She smiled inwardly. Not that she'd have the robe on for long anyway.

A flash of movement at the corner of her vision pulled her from her reverie. Someone was rushing her! By the time she turned, all she could see were two menacing eyes staring back at her through a black mask. She opened her mouth to scream at the same time she was pushed over the railing.

* * * * *

A scream penetrated the deepest reaches of Christian's mind. Having fallen asleep on the couch in his study, he woke with a jolt, holding his breath, listening. Had it been a dream? But no, he heard the shouts being ordered by Jared to get a doctor.

The hair on the back of his neck stood on end. Good lord, what now?

Racing out into the hallway, he looked toward the stairway where half a dozen servants huddled around someone. His stomach clenched into a tight knot as he walked toward the group, his gaze not wavering from the still body lying at their feet. From the little he could see, he knew it to be a woman by the shoes. Alex? Hearing his heartbeat pounding in his ears, he approached the gathering to find Alex lying flat on her back, a huge gash on her head bleeding profusely.

"Is she alive?"

"She has a pulse," Jared replied, his white pallor belying his calm voice.

"How did this happen?"

Jared shrugged. "I don't know, my lord. I believe she fell. Perhaps she slid down the banister again. It's a miracle she's even alive. I don't know how anyone could survive such a fall."

I believe she fell. His heart gave a jolt. Had she really fallen, or could someone have pushed her? Why would someone hurt her though? Going down on his knees, Christian looked her over, hoping that the gash to the head was the only injury she'd suffered.

Though that alone could very well prove fatal.

An hour later Christian paced the floor waiting for the doctor to finish his examination. It was all he could do to stop himself from asking what was taking so damn long. Reginald kept him busy by talking about trivial matters. Yet he welcomed the conversation, if only to free his mind from what was happening behind the closed door.

Further thoughts were cut off when the door to the room opened and the bald-headed doctor stepped out with bag in hand. His warm smile put Christian immediately at ease.

"I can't explain how she survived such a fall. She will need a lot of rest and will be sore for some time, but other than a sprained wrist and a concussion, she is quite unharmed. She should pull through with no trouble. Quite strong-willed, that one. Told me she was getting out of bed no matter what I said."

He laughed under his breath. "Thank goodness the laudanum works quickly. She is already asleep. I've stitched the deep gash on her head, but the wound will need to be cleaned often, so I've left a bottle of antiseptic, along with some laudanum on the bedside table. Make sure *that* is used sparingly…

"Although, it looks as though you could use a little yourself. Those dark smudges under your eyes tell me you're not sleeping, and you've dropped a stone since last we met."

"I'll see that he gets some rest, doctor." Jared arrived to escort the doctor to the door. "I have been warning him that if he continues to lose weight, I shall have to feed him myself."

The doctor laughed. "Very well, then. I expect you to look fit when next I come to check on our patient. If you don't, I may tell Jared to keep you under lock and key until you get some rest."

"Thanks for the warning, doctor." Christian extended his hand to the pleasant man. "And for coming so quickly. I am in your debt."

The doctor shook his hand firmly and flashed another warm smile before exiting the room with Jared. Christian passed by Reginald into the adjoining room.

He stopped short seeing Alexandria lying in bed, her head bandaged. For the first time she looked fragile to him, so unlike the outgoing, rambunctious woman he was accustomed to. Sitting on the edge of the bed, he ran his fingertips across her temple, her cheek, her jaw, and her lips.

The doctor was right. How had she survived such a fall? It didn't seem possible, but he was grateful all the same. What would he have done had she not lived through that fall? How had this woman become so dear to him in so short a time? Alex's brows furrowed, and he wondered what she dreamt of. He leaned over and kissed her. She smiled a little. His heart soared.

Cold air filled the room. Christian got up to check the doors and windows. He frowned. The room was shut up tight, and he could find no drafts. He glanced at Alex. She continued to sleep, her breathing slow and even.

His gaze scanned every inch of the room, but there was no one. "Hello?" What was he doing? He shook his head. Was it just the lingering effects of the alcohol? Running his fingers through his hair, he sat down in the chair, and yet he still couldn't shake the feeling that someone watched him.

* * * * *

Alex watched Mimi beneath lowered lashes. For four days the woman had been caring for her. Though Mimi had been nothing but kind, Alex wondered if it was an act. After all, why would she have taken Devon's journal if she were not the murderer?

"You don't have to take care of me. I'm fine."

"Nonsense," Mimi replied, handing Alex a cup of hot tea.

Looking into the steaming cup, she couldn't help but wonder if the tea had been laced with arsenic. A terrible thought, but, given that someone had pushed her over the banister, probably legitimate.

Bringing the tea to her lips, Alex pretended to take a drink before setting it on the bedside table. Pushing the covers aside, she stood and walked toward the window. Where had Christian been these past four days?

"You should not be up, Alex." Mimi stood, hands planted on hips. "The doctor said you need at least one week's worth of bed rest."

"I'm going crazy lying in this bed day in and day out."

She leaned her forehead against the cool window. The skies were overcast, the clouds dark and full, looking like any minute it would open up and pour. Alex scanned the immaculately manicured grounds, hoping to see Christian, but there was no one about. She turned back to the maid. "How is his lordship?"

Mimi's brows lifted. "Fine. Concerned about you. He comes by everyday to check on you, but you're always asleep."

"Only because you're drugging me."

The sides of her mouth curved. "The laudanum will help you sleep and recover."

"It makes me sleep too much."

"Get back in bed. I have to help with preparing tonight's meal. Apparently Abigail has requested roasted duck with a wine sauce made of her brother's favorite Madeira. For dessert she asked for us to prepare baked plum pudding." Mimi sighed heavily. "I shall be so happy to see those two leave."

Knowing Mimi would never leave her alone if she didn't get back in bed, Alex lay back down. "You're not the only one that wants to see the last of those two."

"I shall visit you late this evening. Get some rest now." Mimi closed the door gently behind her.

"I see the princess has awoken from her slumber." Devon appeared, sitting in the chair, his legs crossed at the ankle, his smile bright. "You make a most horrible patient."

"Yes, well, I was never one for hospitals, and I feel like I'm in one now. Mimi keeps an eye on me night and day. Thank God she's helping out Cook this evening, or else I'd have her breathing down my neck." Alex jumped up and went to the dresser. She opened the top drawer and grabbed the journal. "Lookie what I found!"

Devon sat forward in the chair. "My journal."

Alex sat on the edge of the bed and cracked it open. "It doesn't make a lot of sense to go through it, considering the murderer lives in this house."

"I have put you in danger, Alex. I should have known that the murderer was someone in the house."

"Yes, but you also broke my fall. If not for you, I would have died."

He shrugged. "I could not allow you to be hurt."

"So…did you see who pushed me?"

He shook his head. "No, I was on my way to find you when I saw you fall. Fortunately, I was at the right place at the right time."

She handed him the journal. "I found this in Mimi's room."

He thumbed through the book, looking not all surprised that it had been in Mimi's possession. "Mimi is not the person who shoved me, if that's what you're thinking."

"How do you know?"

He closed the book and looked at her, a soft expression on his handsome features. "Because she loved me, and I loved her."

"Were you lovers?" She felt bad for prying, but needed to know the truth.

He shook his head, sadness flashing in his eyes. Or was it regret? "No, but I wanted to be. She is without a doubt the kindest, most giving woman I have ever known. If only she had not been my servant, or anyone else's servant for that matter. If only she had been part of the peerage, I would have married her a long time ago. As it was, I had to make do with watching her grow from awkward girl, to beautiful woman, all along keeping my thoughts—and my hands—to myself."

"She obviously knew how you felt, or else you wouldn't have told me she loved you as well."

He nodded. "We shared looks when she served dinner, or when I'd come upon her in a room she was cleaning, I would find her staring at me, or she would find me staring at her."

"Yet you never acted on your desires?"

"What good would it have done? I would have only ended up hurting her, especially since rumors had been circulating for some time that I was looking for a wife."

She didn't think he'd have to look too hard to find a wife. No doubt he'd had to fight them off with a stick. Kind of like Christian and Abigail. He didn't want her, yet she pushed herself on him. "And were you looking for a wife?"

"Secretly, yes. I wasn't getting younger, and I wanted a wife, and children. I wanted to make sure the Strathmore dynasty lived on."

"No wonder Reginald and Abigail made the trip from France."

He shrugged. "I've little doubt that was the motivation from the beginning, and I know for certain that's why they remain. As with all single titled men of a certain age, my brother will need to marry soon and get an heir, or our lineage will die out. Both Abigail and Reginald know this."

A heaviness centered in her chest. One day Christian would have to marry, and his wife would have to be a member of the peerage. A woman like Abigail. She sighed heavily.

Devon smiled. "You love my brother already, don't you?"

"Yeah, I do."

"You will have to leave here one day, Alex, and then what?"

She shrugged. "I haven't thought about it." She had pushed that thought aside, especially this past week since her relationship with Christian had become physical.

"Perhaps you will have to consider it. You're very close to finding the killer. In my heart I know the knowledge will save Christian, but I must tell you that you will still have to leave here, and Christian will get married and move on with his life."

That was the last thing she wanted to hear. She'd been living a fantasy, complete with her own dashing prince. Deep in her heart she had hoped that her being a servant wouldn't matter…or that she was from a different century. She knew Devon didn't tell her out of malice, but concern.

"I must go and let you rest," Devon said, already fading before her eyes.

Alone now, Alex considered her future. She and Christian did not have a future. She had known that, yet she had given into her desire and slept with him.

A pain squeezed her heart. How would she be able to walk away now? Even when she saved him, and she *would* save him, how could she look into that beloved face and say goodbye?

Chapter Nine

෯

Alex removed the bandage from her head and winced from the pain that shot to her temple. Every muscle in her body ached.

For a week she had lain in bed, waiting patiently as Mimi fawned over her like a mother hen. Though Alex appreciated the woman's kindness, she was at the end of her patience, especially when Mimi suggested she take another spoonful of laudanum just over an hour ago. Being drugged was not a good idea when a killer was loose. There had been a number of times Alex had wanted to ask Mimi about Devon's journal, but she decided waiting until she recuperated would be better. She didn't think Mimi had killed Devon. Sure, the maid might be jealous that Devon was looking for a wife, but murder? She couldn't imagine that. All the same, Alex wanted to wait to confront her.

With candle in hand, Alex tiptoed to the door and opened it slowly. Seeing the hallway clear, she stepped out of her room, shut the door quietly behind her and headed for the doorway Christian had showed her a week ago, a few hours after they'd made love in his study. That night they had planned to make love, but she had been pushed instead. And now she hadn't seen him for an entire week. What kept him from coming to her?

Now she would have to brave the servants' secret staircase to go to him.

The door creaked on its hinges. Alex held her breath, and glanced over her shoulder, half-expecting Jared to be there. When she shut the door behind her, the candle wavered, but thankfully didn't go out. Reminding herself that the stress of being in the dark would be well worth it, she did her relaxation breathing, inhaling through her nose and exhaling out of her mouth.

Cobwebs blocked the way, telling her it had been a long time since any servant had used the stairwell. A glimmer of light shone up ahead and Alex increased her pace. Was that a peephole? Maybe there were peepholes into all the guestrooms so that the servants could check on the guests. Though the room was dimly lit, she recognized it as the guestroom Abigail occupied.

Seeing two bodies in the bed, her stomach clenched. Certainly Christian wasn't sleeping with Abigail? Was that why he hadn't visited her while she was recovering…? Black fury filled her entire body. What if Abigail had seduced Christian? The shock of the possibility that she had lost Christian to that bitch held her immobile, watching, waiting. She gripped the candle tighter, her nails digging into the wax. When Abigail's throaty laughter rang out, her lover shh'd her, putting a finger to her lips. Alex squinted, trying in get a better look.

The man rolled onto Abigail, his dark hair shining in the light. Alex's blood pulsed in her veins, as the man kissed a path from Abigail's lips and disappeared beneath the sheets. A moment later Abigail's legs fell apart and her cries filled the room as her lover went down on her. The woman's intense moans spoke of her lover's skill.

That asshole!

Alex would kill Christian herself! Unable to move, Alex watched like a voyeur as Abigail reached climax, her head rolling back and forth on the pillow. "Fuck me," Abigail said, the words a plea.

The man tossed the sheets aside. It wasn't Christian.

Her heart missed a beat.

It was *Reginald*.

The exultation quickly gave way to disgust. They were sister and brother, how could they?

Or were they really sister and brother?

Abigail's moans filled the room as Reginald positioned his cock at her entrance and took her. The two kissed passionately — Abigail's hands moving down her lover's back, slapping his ass, then pulling him tighter to her.

Alex had seen enough. Trembling, she continued up the steps, taking care to be quiet should she be discovered by the two. Why would they pretend to be brother and sister? Were they out to swindle Christian? Should she tell Christian what she saw, or would it be better to withhold the information and see how things played out? Maybe it would work to her advantage if no one else knew. That way she could study the two. Yet if Christian knew then the two of them could work together.

She had walked up what felt like six flights of steps when she came to the end. Tired, every muscle screaming, she lifted the latch on the door she assumed to be Christian's chamber.

She pushed on the door, and it gave a great creak.

She winced at the sound. So much for surprising Christian.

Uneasy, not knowing what to expect, she entered the room. Shutting the door, she walked to the bed where Christian lay still asleep despite the noise. A book rested on his chest. The light on the side table flickered, illuminating his handsome face and impressive body. How boyish he seemed in his sleep. Her gaze shifted lower, over his wide chest and chiseled abdomen. She almost hated to wake him. Sitting on the edge of the bed, she ran a hand over a flat nipple. He didn't move. Growing more brazen in her attempt to wake him, her hand drifted lower, over his abdomen, circling his navel, and following the line of dark hair that disappeared beneath the sheet. His cock grew, tenting the sheet and she smiled, looking up to find him watching her.

"Witch." He pulled her on top of him. "What are you doing out of bed?"

Relief and excitement bubbled within her. "I couldn't sleep. I'm restless, so I thought I'd come up and see if you wanted to play."

He wound a lock of her hair around his finger. "I am delighted you came to see me, but I'm not certain you should be here. The doctor might not approve."

She considered withholding her information about Abigail and Reginald until later, but didn't feel right keeping it from him. Perhaps the information could wait until later. His hard body felt wonderful beneath hers. His hard cock pressing against her belly reminded her of the week they'd been apart. But if she didn't say something now, she would fret about it. Like a kid with a secret, she blurted, "I have to tell you something."

"What?"

"I saw Reginald and Abigail making love in her room."

He frowned. "Alex, are you sure you are well?"

"I saw them just now, on my way up here. I passed by her quarters, and I saw them."

He put her from him and scrambled to his feet. "Are you certain it was Reginald?"

"Positive."

She could see the wheels turning in his mind. "Come on." Throwing his legs over the side of the bed, he got up and walked bare-assed to the door. Desire warmed every inch of her.

"At least put your pants on."

He went for his robe, the muscles beneath his golden skin moving with the slight movement. Maybe she should have kept her mouth shut. At least until they'd made love.

"Are you coming?" He grabbed the candelabra.

She held onto his waist as they made their way down the stairs. Abigail's cries carried out to the stairwell and Reginald's groans followed. Christian bent and looked in the peephole. The muscles in his back tensed under her hand. A moment later, he motioned for her to head back up the steps.

Safely in his room, he ran a hand through his hair. "Well, I think it is safe to assume the two are not brother and sister."

"And it's also safe to assume that they are trying to swindle you. Why else would Reginald play chaperone for his sister, and push you two together at every opportunity?"

"They want the Strathmore title, and with Devon out of the way, all they need to do is to dispose of me, and they shall have it. They are here to kill me."

Unable to stand the pain in his eyes, Alex went to him, sat on his lap and kissed him. "I'm sorry, Christian."

He cupped her face with his hands, his gaze searching hers. "I am so grateful you are all right. Reginald knew that you and I were lovers, so he tried to kill you too." He ran his thumb over her bottom lip. "I shall enjoy killing him very much."

"Why don't you let the constable take care of it?"

"You would be surprised how money and influence can sway a person. I will not take the chance."

She could see the need for vengeance in his eyes. It made her uneasy. "Promise me you won't put yourself in danger."

His gaze shifted from hers, lower. "Look, your gown is a mess. Let me help you off with it."

At the obvious change of subject, Alex frowned. He was trying to distract her by getting her naked and making love to her. Christian just smiled and untied her robe. The garment pooled at her feet.

Stripping off his robe, displaying his fully erect cock, he took her by the hand and pulled her down on the bed, enfolding her in his arms. "I'm so relieved you are well. You have no idea how I worried about you. It seemed every time I came to visit, you were always sleeping."

She closed her eyes, listening to the pounding of his heart against her ear. All the uneasiness of the past week disappeared, replaced with a need that consumed her.

His fingers grazed her back, sending shards of pleasure throughout her body. "Mimi had me drugged."

Laughing, he slid down her body, his mouth covering a nipple. His tongue swirled, tugged, causing an ache deep inside her vagina. He stroked the delicate skin where her groin and thighs met, her hips moved against his hand. His fingers worked magic, drawing a heated path over her dewy folds, his thumb finding her clit. "You're so wet for me, Alex. I love when you come."

His words worked like an aphrodisiac, pushing her toward the edge. Her body tightened; a pulsing throb began. His thumb stroked harder. The orgasm rocked her, taking her breath for a heart-stopping moment as she rode out the wonderfully wicked sensations.

His lips left her breasts, traveling down, over her stomach, laving her navel, before moving lower still. Alex's breath left her in a rush as he stroked her nether lips with his tongue, lifting the tiny nub before sucking it. Christian looked up at her, his eyes heavy-lidded. He knew how crazy with need she was. She reached for his head, her fingers running through the silky dark tresses. Electricity raced along her spine at the sight of his tongue giving her such wicked pleasure. The feel of his soft hair against her thighs and fingers, the look in his eyes as he now watched her in turn, made her burn from the inside out. The sides of his mouth curved just slightly and then with hands beneath her ass, he lifted her to him. His tongue flicked over and over, while he held her hips tight so that she couldn't squirm away from his ministrations.

Her heart pounded, her body tightened until she felt like she would spiral out of control. Nothing had ever felt this good.

Moments later she lay with eyes closed, her butt firmly back on the sheets. "*That* was so good."

For an answer, he kissed her and entered her in one fluid motion. Then, he waited, holding very still, as if to let her feel every inch of his hard cock pulsing within her, claiming her. She moved her hands eagerly over his strong shoulders, down his back and waist, and cupped his high, tight ass, urging him to deepen his strokes.

He did not disappoint. The slow tempo built with each intense thrust, bringing her to the brink of orgasm. It seemed he knew just when she was ready to come, because each time she drew near he stopped, kissed her tenderly, then began to move again…slowly.

Taking matters into her own hands, Alex kissed his jaw, his neck, before slipping the tip of her tongue around the ridge of his ear. His pace quickened and she smiled to herself, biting his lobe before stroking his ear with her tongue.

Her orgasm came fast, turning her inside out. She felt like she could soar with the birds. Christian followed behind, his moans filling the chamber.

* * * * *

Alex opened her eyes to the sliver of light that spilled in through the window. She smiled to herself, recalling last night's lovemaking. She and Christian had made love all night long. Afterward, while she lay in his arms, they had talked about Reginald and Abigail. Whenever she asked what he planned to do about the two, he would just grin and tell her she would find out soon enough.

Someone cleared a throat. Embarrassed, she looked around. Alex gasped and pulled up the sheet around her. Devon sat in a chair five feet away, a devilish grin on his face. "Well, what a little vixen we've turned out to be."

Glancing over her shoulder to make sure Christian still slept soundly, she put her finger to her lips. "Hand me my robe," she whispered, extending her hand, waiting for Devon, who, with grin in place, picked up the robe and handed it to her.

"Turn around."

He rolled his eyes but looked the other way. Alex slid from the bed, put her robe on and then motioned for Devon to follow her to the opposite side of the room. Hopefully far enough way that Christian could not hear.

"You must tell him."

Alex turned. "Tell him what?"

He lifted a brow. "That you will need to leave here as soon as this is resolved. That you come from the future, and that you'll have to leave."

Why did he keep reminding her of when she would leave here? She wished she could forget that this would not last. That one day she would return to her own time and this would be nothing but a memory. True, she had known she would have to leave once the murderer was found and Christian was safe, but she hadn't expected to fall in love with the man she had come to protect.

Christian heard voices. He opened his eyes and found Alex standing in the middle of the room, talking to someone. The problem was he couldn't see another person in the room. As the seconds ticked by he became increasingly aware that Alex was talking to herself.

What had Jared said a few days ago? *Miss Drake is constantly talking to herself. There is something very wrong with that young woman!*

Was she mad…or did she also feel a presence?

"Devon, this is madness." The hair on the back of Christian's neck stood on end.

Dear God, could Alex see his brother? Had she all along? Christian followed Alex's line of vision, hoping against hope to see Devon for himself. Nothing.

"He'll never believe me. Now go away. I need to get downstairs before Mimi finds me gone."

"What won't I believe?"

Devon had just vanished when the question came from Christian. Alex whirled around. "I—"

"Who are you talking to, Alex?" Christian sat up on an elbow.

She opened her mouth. How much had he heard? This did not look good. "Sorry, just talking to myself again."

He pursed his lips together. "Why do you speak to yourself so often?"

She shrugged, her gaze shifting from his, down his body, hoping the bold stare would invite sex, and distract him. Just as she'd hoped, her gaze made his cock jerk and twitch. He wanted her again.

"Come here." He gave her a knowing smile.

She dropped the robe, and walked slowly to the bed.

His eyes darkened as she climbed on the bed and crawled up his body, stopping to kiss the plum-sized head of his cock. "Do you mind if I try something?"

A dark brow lifted.

"You are in charge, Miss Drake."

The sides of her mouth lifted in an irresistible smile. "Anything?"

"Okay." She jumped off the bed, went to his drawer and pulled out a couple of pair of stockings. With devilish intent burning in her eyes, she went to the foot of the bed, and grabbed one of his legs. Carefully and with a skill that surprised him, she tied his foot to the footboard, and then proceeded to anchor the other foot as well. Next, she moved to his arms, and didn't stop until he was tied securely, spread eagle on his bed.

"Oh, and last but not least." She strode to the door and locked it. "No interruptions."

Crawling onto the bed, she positioned herself between his spread legs. She could hear his quick intake of breath as she stroked the insides of his thighs with her fingertips. Her fingers splayed on his thighs, she lowered her head to lick the tiny bead of moisture from his cockhead. "You taste so good," she said, before taking him into her mouth.

His heart hammered loud in his chest at her ministrations. Never had he been so hard or so excited. Already his sac lifted, ready to pour his seed into her mouth. He shifted his hips and she sat up. "Don't move." She gazed intensely down at his throbbing cock. Her hands wandered between his thighs, then took hold of his sac, finding the sensitive patch on his scrotum, stroking it.

She dipped her head again, taking him into her mouth. Sucking him, laving him, her tongue running along the ridge and around the head of his cock drove him mad with desire. He tested the bonds that held him, wanting desperately to feel her, to take her beneath him and pound into her until she screamed for release.

But she would not have it.

His body pulsed, his cock strained, and his sac tightened. Still she suckled and teased, until he could take it no longer. She gave a long deep draw, and with a low groan he spewed his seed into her hot mouth.

Covered with sweat, he opened his eyes to find her sitting on his thighs, smiling mischievously, a drop of his semen still on her lips.

She didn't touch him, but rather cupped her own breasts, running the nipples between thumbs and forefingers. She licked her lips, and trailed one hand down her stomach, to the patch of curls at the apex of her thighs, then delved into her slick folds. His cock stirred and she smiled.

Christian swallowed hard. Excitement pulsed within him, making him hard again already. She ran a finger over the tiny nub of sensitive skin, circling it, her hips moving. Her lips curved into a seductive smile. He strained against the bonds, desperate to touch her.

"Alex, please," he pleaded, his voice gruff with unspent passion.

"Please what?" She rubbed herself against his cock.

"Untie me."

"What fun would that be?"

"Why don't you untie me and find out."

She straddled him. "No," she said, sinking down on his cock, just taking the head inside her. He lifted his hips, and this time she didn't stop him. She gasped, taking all of him. Sweat beaded his brows as she rotated her hips, moving with slow, deliberate movements.

She leaned forward, offering her breast to him. He lifted his head as far as the bonds would allow and took an elongated nipple into his mouth. Her tempo increased, moving along his cock in a frenzy. He suckled harder. Planting a hand on the headboard for leverage, she rode him mercilessly, her free hand clutching his head, pulling him closer to her breast.

God, she would be the death of him. He loved it!

Her honeyed sheath tightened around his cock, and she ground against him, her cries filling the chamber, and setting off an orgasm that left him trembling.

Chapter Ten

ഊ

Christian put down his paper the moment Reginald and Abigail entered the dining room. An image of the two making love the previous night came unheeded.

Reginald was ever the gentleman as he pulled out the chair for his *sister*. Abigail, looking the part of the virgin in pale blue silk, smiled prettily at Christian.

These two who had made themselves welcome in his home, had more than likely killed Devon…and they had hoped to hang the blame on him. No doubt they planned to make his own death look like an accident or perhaps a suicide. No wonder Reginald had always been slinking around corners, constantly watching him, appearing out of nowhere, asking him questions about business and investment ventures.

Christian smiled at Abigail. "Cousin, you look especially beautiful this morning. It makes me realize just how distracted I have been of late. Perhaps I can remedy my negligence by taking you on a ride."

Triumph glittered in her eyes as she glanced across the table at Reginald, then back to Christian. Reginald sat up taller, and nodded. "I think that is a fabulous idea."

"I thought you would approve," Christian murmured before taking a sip of coffee.

Throughout the meal Christian watched the two cast glances at each other. How had he not noticed before that they were lovers? There was nothing brotherly about the way Reginald watched Abigail. Likewise for Abigail and the way she looked at Reginald. Christian smiled inwardly. How he would enjoy their downfall.

"Reginald, I know you have made it clear that Abigail is looking for a husband, but what of yourself? Is there a certain someone who has caught your eye?"

Reginald, who had been ready to bite into a piece of ham, set his fork down. "I have not found the right woman as of yet."

"I know many women, quite wealthy in fact, who would love to be married to a Frenchman such as yourself. Perhaps you would like me to invite them to Radborne Manor? A small dinner party perhaps?"

Abigail had gone still as a statue as she waited for Reginald to respond.

Reginald flushed. "I would not want you to go to the trouble for me."

"It would be no trouble at all. In fact, it would be my pleasure."

Reginald shifted in his chair. "Very well then, cousin. Thank you."

The rest of the meal took place in silence. Abigail appeared to have lost her appetite, as she pushed food around the plate.

"How is Alexandria?" Reginald finally asked, taking a drink of his tea.

"She is doing quite well. In fact, I hear on good authority she is growing restless. I may just have to have her tied to the bed in order to keep her there." Christian grinned, memories of the night past filling his mind. He would get back at Alexandria, tie her to his bed, and ravage her, just as she had ravaged him. His blood stirred at the memory. Never in his life had a woman excited him the way she did.

But for now, he must focus on the two swindlers before him. Christian pushed back his chair. "Well, I will change into riding attire and meet you at the stables in one hour." With a nod he left the two and headed straight for his room.

He changed quickly, then took the servants' staircase down to Abigail's room. Already he could hear Reginald's voice.

"We have succeeded, my pet." When Christian looked through the knothole, he saw Reginald take Abigail in his arms, swinging her about.

Abigail grinned. "We are so close, I can taste it. I only wish…"

"Now I do not want to see a frown upon that gorgeous face of yours." Reginald turned her about and began to unbutton her dress. The gown fell in a puddle at her feet. He stripped her of her petticoat, shift and corset, leaving nothing but pink knee-high stockings and garters. He unbuttoned his pants, his cock springing forth and Abigail gasped.

She took a step from him, her bottom lip jutting out. "He intends to introduce you to other women…"

Reginald looked down at his erection. "My heart, and all else, belongs to you and you alone."

Abigail sighed dramatically and went into his arms. "I cannot bear the thought of you with another woman."

"But I must bear the thought of you in Strathmore's arms. Keep your chin up, darling. This is the moment we've waited for. You will seduce him, and he will fall helplessly in love with you." He lifted her and backed her up to the wall. With a hard thrust, he entered her. "We will be richer than we ever dreamed."

"Yes, but I do not want to touch another man," Abigail said on a moan.

"Nor can I endure the image of you with him." Reginald's voice was firm, his strokes fast. "I am Strathmore's only living heir, and once he is dead, I will inherit, but that could take some time."

Christian's heart skipped a beat hearing his suspicion about the two murderers confirmed.

"Could we not just kill him now?"

"Soon, princess, soon."

Moans and sighs filled the next minutes as the pair came to climax together. Reginald buttoned his pants, and then helped Abigail into her riding habit.

"Unfortunately the household is jittery after Alexandria's accident. I cannot believe she survived such a fall. I should have pushed harder, as I did with Devon. Of course I had a running start then, and the wrought-iron fence worked to my advantage."

The blood roared in Christian's ears. It was all he could do not to pull out his pistol and kill them on the spot.

"We will wait until things calm down a bit. He is taken with you, so it stands to reason he will no longer ask us to leave. We must make sure that nothing can be traced back to us, just as we did when Alexandria fell from the stairwell."

"Come, you don't want to keep Strathmore waiting."

"I love you." Abigail wrapped her arms around Reginald's neck, kissing him passionately.

Christian took the steps up to his room two at a time, his blood coursing through his veins. He had all the information he needed to charge them with the murder of his brother and the attempted murder of Alex. Sitting down, he quickly wrote all that he'd just heard. He sealed it with red wax, then rang for Jared.

* * * * *

What was he up to?

Alexandria watched from the window as Christian and Abigail rode out, leaving Reginald to watch after them. The man's hands were in his pockets, a gleeful smile on his face as he made his way back to the manor.

Reginald had killed Devon and he would kill Christian. Now it was up to Christian to handle it his way.

The moment Reginald entered the house, Jared started for the stables. Within minutes Michael took off on horseback, riding like the devil was on his heels.

Letting the curtain fall back into place, Alex knew that Christian had come to the same realization as she. She wished Christian would have told her what he'd intended. Despite tying him to the bed and teasing him into a stupor, she'd not been able to get anything out of him. He'd fallen asleep without giving her so much as the slightest clue, and she'd made for her room using the servants' exit, so that Mimi wouldn't sound the alarm on finding her out of bed.

A knock sounded at the door, and Alex jumped back into bed, pulling the covers up over her just as the door opened.

"Alexandria?" Reginald said, a moment before he popped his head in. "Are you awake?"

Pretending she'd just awakened, Alex squinted and sat up against the headboard. "Only just."

He smiled, motioned to the chair. "May I?"

"Of course."

He took a seat, his gaze taking in the small room. The man had not said two words to her before, so she was somewhat intrigued that he had now sought her out. Especially since he tried to kill her… "How are you feeling?"

"Very well, thank you."

"I am amazed at your swift recovery. The doctor said it was nothing short of a miracle that you survived."

No thanks to you, you bastard. She nodded, forcing a smile. "I'm most fortunate."

"Could I get you anything?" he asked, his gaze shifting from her face to her breasts.

The pig! Was he actually trying to seduce her? Did he think her that stupid? She lifted the sheet to her chin.

"No, I'm fine." She tried to get the image of him and Abigail making love out of her mind, but it kept coming back.

How would he react if he knew that she knew the truth about them? Wanting to see him squirm, she asked, "Where is Abigail?"

His gaze lifted to hers. "She has gone on a ride with Strathmore."

"And you didn't follow?"

His lips quirked. "Strathmore wanted to be alone with Abigail—"

"And that doesn't upset you?"

"Should it?" His voice had a sharp edge to it.

Sensing his agitation, Alex smiled inwardly. "Well, with you being her big brother and all…"

Reginald shifted in his seat. "Yes, well, I trust my cousin explicitly. " He sat forward in his chair. "He would not harm one hair on her head." He brushed a curl out of Alex's face as he spoke.

Alex flinched at the contact, but didn't move. His gaze searched her face and he lowered his head to hers. She pulled away. "What are you doing?"

He blinked as though slapped. "I think you are beautiful, Alexandria. I have seen the way you look at me, the heated stares."

Dear God he had to be joking? He actually thought she was buying this act?

Thankfully, the door opened and Mimi appeared with tray in hand, her shock obvious as she backed out of the room. Alex threw her a desperate look and Mimi stayed, shutting the door behind her.

Reginald jumped away, his face flushing.

"I have brought you some breakfast." Mimi placed the tray on the bedside table. "Would you care for a bath after you eat?"

"Very much so." Alex smiled, then turned to Reginald. "Perhaps we can finish this conversation later?"

A tight smile spread across Reginald's face. "I would like that very much."

He left and Mimi shut the door behind him. "What was he doing in here?"

Alex released a breath. "He actually tried to kiss me."

Mimi cringed. "He makes me uneasy, the way he is always watching after Abigail. Do you know that one morning I went to clean her quarters and when I entered, he was in bed with her, his nightclothes on."

"Really?"

"Yes, and when I came in he jumped off the bed as though it had caught fire. Abigail blushed to the roots of her hair, and Reginald told me that his sister had a horrible nightmare in the middle of the night and he had slept with her." Mimi lifted her brows. "Quite odd, wouldn't you say?"

"Quite." Alex glanced out the window, wishing she had the technology from her time to call Christian and find out his whereabouts.

She had a bad feeling that things were just about to get worse.

* * * * *

Christian and Abigail stopped for a rest at the river's edge. After helping Abigail down from her mount, he kept his hands on her waist and guided her to a clearing. There, he lay out a blanket, motioned for her to sit while he unpacked the wine and two glasses.

He filled the glasses to the brim with a potent wine, and handed her one. Abigail took a long swallow, licked her lips and smiled. "What a beautiful place this is."

Christian reached out and stroked her jaw with his thumb. "A beautiful place for a beautiful woman."

Abigail took another long swallow, her gaze fastened on the river.

Christian smiled to himself. At this rate, she'd be drunk in no time. "I cannot apologize enough for my negligence of late. I want you to know that I will make it up to you from this moment on."

He leaned forward, kissed her lightly on the cheek, and then filled her glass again. "Tell me about Paris." If he could just keep her busy and drinking…"I know my brother adored the city. He often spoke fondly of his time there."

She took a few more gulps of wine. "Paris is an amazing city. It is a beautiful home, right on the river Seine."

"How long have you and Reginald lived there?"

Her brows furrowed. "Let me see. Two years."

He nodded, poured her more wine and watched with relief as she gulped it down.

Lying back on his elbows he listened as she told him of Paris, the sights, the architecture, the times she and Reginald spent. At every opportunity Christian refilled her glass.

Within half an hour she began to slur, her words coming quickly, running together. Pleased by her chattiness, he nodded in interest, acting the ardent suitor.

"You are not drinking," she said, giggling. "I think you mean to get me drunk."

Smiling, he leaned into her and kissed her softly on the lips. "Perhaps, but you cannot blame me. There is not a man in all of England who could resist your charms, sweet Abigail."

For a moment her guard slipped and he saw uncertainty in her eyes, but then she took another drink of wine and almost toppled the near-empty bottle upon setting the glass down. She leaned into him, her hand coming dangerously close to the pistol in his jacket pocket. "You have no idea how long I have waited for you to take notice of me."

"I thought you cared for Devon."

She blushed. "Only because you showed no interest." She kissed his jaw, his neck.

It was all he could do not to push her off of him. "You have no head for wine, my dear." His words sounded harsher than he'd intended. Her eyes widened in apparent distress, so he softened the words with a kiss to her cheek.

Knowing he had a part to play, he kissed her on the mouth, and immediately she opened for him, her tongue stroking his, urging him to deepen the kiss. Pulling him tight to her, she moaned loudly, as though she were trying convince herself that she enjoyed his touch. "Take me, Christian. Take me now."

He pulled away, looking down into her flushed face. Her eyes were half-closed, her lips opened, her gaze shifting to his lips once more. "Please…"

This was almost too easy. He sat up, handed her the wine glass, while he worked the laces of her boots, the task taking far longer than it should have. He stalled for time. Thankfully she seemed not to notice. She swallowed the wine in one mouthful and fell back blissfully on the blanket. Christian tossed the boots aside, then massaged her feet. She moaned low in her throat, and even sighed when he advanced further up her leg.

"That is heavenly," she whispered, looking up at him with half-closed eyes. "Come to me, Christian. Make love to me." The words were a plea, and the heated look in her eyes made him wonder if the wine had worked better than intended. She looked like she did desire him.

"In due time, my sweet."

Her eyes crossed as she watched him.

"Christian, there are two of you."

Leaning over her, he kissed her ankle, making a trail up her leg, to the inside of her knee. She writhed beneath him, sighing. "Mmm, that feels delicious. Do not stop, whatever you do."

Christian heard the rustling of brush coming from nearby. Hopefully it was Andrew, the groom, come to be another set of ears. Now if only Abigail would start confessing.

"Tell me, how long have you and Reginald known one another?"

"Mmmm, two years now."

"Where did you meet?" He continued kissing her, his lips tracing a path up the inside of her thigh. Her legs spread wider, her hips tilting. "In Paris…exhibit."

"At an exhibit?"

She nodded. "Yes, I love painting, as does Reginald. Do you like painting, Christ—"

"Yes, I do enjoy painting. Perhaps one day I could paint you?"

Eyes still closed, she smiled. "Oh, I would like that very much."

Running his fingertips along her lower leg, he congratulated himself as her eyes closed. "Reginald, I want to go home now. I am very tired."

Reginald? Good, she was growing careless.

"Come, pet, let me take you home."

"Make love to me again, Reggie, please."

"When we get home I shall, my precious, of that I promise."

She smiled then, and fell off to sleep.

Christian glanced at the empty wine bottle with a smile.

Chapter Eleven

ဆာ

Alex swallowed a gasp and slid further into the tub as Devon appeared from nowhere. "Devon!"

"Sorry," he said, a mischievous grin on his face. "I must share the good news! A Bow Street Runner is on his way here. It seems that our killer has been found."

"Reginald."

He nodded. "Indeed, and you were the one who discovered him."

"Where is Christian now?"

"I do not know. The last time I saw him, he was headed off with Abigail on horseback. However, I do know that he requested wine and two glasses, so I have little doubt he plans to get Abigail foxed."

Alex wished he hadn't gone alone. Someone needed to have his back just in case Reginald pulled something. After all, the man couldn't be trusted. And how did they know it was just Reginald and Abigail? What if someone else, possibly from the manor, worked with them?

Unable to shake the bad vibe, she asked Devon, "Is Reginald still here?"

"I believe so."

"The last thing we need is Reginald riding out to find them. We already know what he's capable of."

"Wait just a second," Devon said, walking through the wall.

While he was gone, Alex got out of the tub, dried herself off and put on a robe. After she'd brushed out her hair, she put on drawers, a chemise and a skirt and shirt. She had one boot on when Devon appeared. "Reginald is gone."

Alex could feel the blood drain from her face. "You don't think he would have gone after them, do you?"

Devon shook his head. "I don't know."

Sliding her foot in the boot, she laced it and raced out of the manor, her thoughts in turmoil. Why hadn't someone followed Christian to see to his safety? Michael had taken off, but where had he been going? "Come with me." She ran down the stairs and out the front door.

"Have you ever ridden?" Devon raced past her to the stable door. He tossed it open.

She shook her head. "Never."

"Dear God."

"Thanks for your encouragement."

Devon proved a great help with the horse, who obviously could see Devon since it nudged him and neighed. "Jezebel is my horse. I cannot tell you how I've missed her," he said, mounting and pulling Alex before him. "Take the reins in your hands, but hold them loosely. I'll do the rest."

They ate up the miles, the wind whipping Alex's hair and apparently hitting Devon square in the face, since he finally wrapped the length and tucked it in the collar of her blouse.

She could feel Devon's legs behind her, his broad chest securely against her back, giving her comfort against the fear that they'd run straight into a hole…and fly ass over teakettle from the huge gray. Or worse.

They had ridden hard for half an hour when Devon abruptly reined in. Alex glanced over her shoulder to find Devon looking off to the right. "Over by the river." He tugged on the reins and they galloped toward the thicket of trees.

Tapping on her shoulder, he put a finger to his lips, signaling silence. Helping her down, he tied the horse to a tree, then made their way along a small dirt path.

Alex's heart pounded. Too late she realized she didn't have a weapon. What good would she do Christian, especially if Reginald were here and had a gun?

Devon pulled her down to the ground beside him. He pointed, and Alex saw Christian and Abigail. The woman's gown was hiked up to thigh level, and Christian sat back on his elbows, watching the river.

Devon nodded toward the right, and just then Reginald made his way into the clearing, a rock in hand. Just as she'd feared, he hadn't been able to take the thought of Christian and Abigail together. Christian's back was to the man, so he couldn't see him coming.

Before Alex could blink, Devon flew across the clearing, knocking down Reginald who fell to the ground with a *whumph.*

Instantly Christian was on his feet, his eyes wide as he looked at Reginald, then the rock. Reginald scrambled up, looking about him wildly. "What in God's name?"

"What are you about, Reginald?" Christian asked, his voice low and even.

Reginald's gaze fell on Abigail, then the empty wine bottle. "What have you done to her?"

"Nothing she didn't want me to do."

"You lying bastard," Reginald said, his face turning bright red. Reaching into his pocket, Reginald pulled out a pistol. "I would have preferred using a rock, for it would have been less messy and easier to explain, but this will work as well."

Christian stood, removed the gun from his jacket. "You won't get away with it. Even if I am killed, there is already a letter en route to Detective Thacker that points to you as the killer. And your lover here," he glanced at Abigail, "will hang with you."

Fear flashed in Reginald's eyes. "You lie."

Alex crawled through the brush, her heart pounding with every second. From the corner of her eye she saw a movement in the brush. Andrew, the groom had hunched down behind some brush, a rifle trained on Reginald.

Abigail came awake, just then. Her eyes widened as she apparently realized what was happening. She grabbed the empty bottle and stood on unsteady legs.

"She is innocent of murder." Reginald took a step closer to Christian.

Abigail lifted the bottle over her head, ready to break it over Christian's. "Watch out, Christian," Alex yelled, and Devon brought Christian to the ground. A shot rang out and Abigail fell, blood spreading over the bodice of her gown.

"My pet," Reginald cried, running to Abigail's side. "My God, what have I done?"

Alex ran into the clearing, right into Christian's arms.

Reginald looked up at them, hatred on his face, which turned quickly to fear when he glanced just to their right where Devon stood. "It *cannot* be!"

Christian's arms tightened around Alex.

Scrambling on all fours, Reginald reached for the gun and shot at Devon. Christian put Alex behind him. "Reginald, put the gun down."

"How can he be alive?"

Confused, Christian took a step toward him. "Put the gun down."

Reginald glanced at Devon, then Abigail's body. Reginald turned the gun on Christian. "I will kill you both."

Andrew stepped out from the brush, rifle at the ready. Devon took a step toward Reginald and the gun shook in Reginald's hand. "You stay back. Stay back, do you hear!"

Bewildered, Christian turned to Alex. "Who is he talking to?"

"Devon's here." Alex saw the confusion on Christian's face, and wished there would have been a way to prepare him.

Reginald jumped. "You see him as well?"

Alex nodded. "I always could."

"It's over now, Reginald. Abigail is dead." Christian's voice remained calm.

Reginald flinched as though he'd been struck. "No! It can *not* be."

Christian motioned toward Abigail's still body. "Look for yourself."

He fell to his knees beside his lover, taking her in his arms, yet still holding the gun. "My precious, wake. Wake, my precious." Tears fell down his cheeks onto Abigail's pale face.

Without warning, Reginald lifted the gun to his temple and pulled the trigger.

Alex covered her eyes with her hands. Christian pulled her into his arms, shielding her from the gruesome sight. He ran his hand down her back in a soothing gesture. "It's over now."

They held each other. She closed her eyes and took solace in listening to the beating of his heart. Thank God he was still alive.

"Andrew, return to the manor and bring back a wagon." Christian waited until Andrew left before he lifted Alex's chin with his fingers.

"Devon *is* here, isn't he?"

"Yes."

Christian swallowed hard. "So I wasn't just imagining?"

"No, you weren't imagining."

He ran a trembling hand down his face. "Why can you see him, yet I cannot?"

"Why don't you ask him? He's standing right next to you."

Tears filled Christian's eyes as he looked from her to the air beside him. "I can feel him," he said, taking a deep breath. "Why can I not see you, Devon, when others can?"

With each second Devon's image became clearer, losing the transparent quality in which she had always seen him. Now he appeared to be flesh and blood just like she and Christian.

"Dev," Christian said, his breath leaving him in a rush. "I cannot believe it." He reached out, and grabbed hold of Devon and embraced him.

Brushing away tears, Alex took a step away, allowing the brothers a moment. How excited Christian appeared. She felt a warm glow flow through her at his happiness.

Christian shook his head. "How? I do not understand."

"Christian, I have been with you all along. I couldn't leave knowing that your life was in danger."

"But how come you did not show yourself to me?"

"I did. Like the time in the library. You saw me then, yet you convinced yourself otherwise. I know how bullheaded you are, so I figured that I would have to take another route."

"Such as?"

"Since no one could see me in this time, I looked for help elsewhere."

He glanced at Alex. "We brought her from the future, Christian. To help you."

She could see him digesting the information. Christian looked at her, his brows furrowed in a frown. Oh dear, was he upset with her? "How is that even possible?"

"Trust me, it is. You knew she was different all along. What you didn't know is that she came through time to help us, to save you."

"Then why did you not bring her back to a time before your murder? She could have saved both of us."

Devon lifted a brow. "Because you know as well as I that we would not have believed her and probably would have had her committed."

Christian frowned. "I still don't—" He sighed. "God, Dev, I miss you."

"I miss you as well, but know that I'll always be with you." He smiled reassuringly. "Now you must listen to me, Christian.

I brought Alex here, but now that she has done what I've asked of her, I must see that she returns to her own time."

Christian dropped his hands from Devon's shoulders. "No!"

"She has done what I asked of her, and now to be fair, I must return her. If she stays, she can never return to her time, ever. She must be willing to give that life up."

Turning to her, Christian pleaded, "Tell him you want to stay."

Could she stay in this time and not live to regret it? Christian cared for her, but he had not once declared his love for her. Yet nor had she. Her mind raced. She hadn't talked to her prescription-drug popping mother for five years, and her father had been nonexistent for the past decade, so he wouldn't miss her at all. The only person who would miss her was Liz. Her partner would probably go crazy wondering what had happened to her. "I wish Liz…"

"I can tell Liz what has happened to you. I can visit her, and put the thought into her mind, that you have traveled through time to find your soulmate. It will be hard for her to understand at first, but in time she will come to accept it, and will make peace with it, just as you will."

"Alex…"

She wanted, no, *needed* to wake up in his arms each morning, have lots of babies, and grow old with him by her side. To return to her own time would be madness. There was nothing waiting for her there. This was her future.

"Alex," Christian blurted, reaching out and taking hold of her hand. "I love you more than I've ever loved anyone. I want us to be together for always. Please stay with me."

He loved her. The declaration filled her with delight and warmth. "I want to stay, but only on one condition."

"Anything," Christian said, tightening his hold on Alex's hand as though he were afraid she'd disappear.

"Marry me."

Relief evident on his features, Christian laughed. "Gladly."

Christian reached out to her and she took his hand. "Let's go home."

Chapter Twelve

ಶಿ

The wedding was a small affair. Just the bride and groom and all twenty servants of Radborne Manor. Alex knew that questions would abound about the wedding, particularly as to her lineage. Christian had thought of everything. She was the daughter of the Count of Kerkenna, from a small island in the Mediterranean. Invitations to balls, soirees and every huge event of the season had come in from the moment the news had hit the papers.

Alex stood from the bath and took the robe Mimi offered. Christian had just returned from business with his solicitor and now waited for her in their bedchamber. "We have prepared a veritable feast for you this evening," Mimi said, a smile on her face. The maid had been glowing these past few weeks since telling Alex that Devon had shown himself to her. It had been a brief moment when Mimi had been preparing for bed. Just after his appearance Mimi had ran into Alex's chambers. *Devon told me that I would see him again. In a time when class and station do not matter. He promised that he would find me, no matter what it took.* Alex grinned at her friend, hoping that Devon would be true to his word and find her again in another lifetime.

Entering the dimly lit chambers, Alex shut the door behind her, telling Mimi she'd see her later. On a nearby table a bottle of wine sat chilling, in the fireplace a fire roared.

Dressed in a robe and a devilish smile, Christian stepped out of the sitting room. "Come here." He opened his arms and she went into them. Closing her eyes she inhaled his masculine scent and smiled up at her husband. How her life had changed in just a few short weeks.

He kissed her lightly. "Let me brush out your hair." He motioned for her to take a seat near the fire. Standing behind her, he brushed her hair while she played with her wedding ring on her finger. The very ring she had found in his jewelry box that day not so long ago. She took the ring off and squinted down at the inscription. It was hard to see by the light of the fire.

"Two hearts forever as one."

Alex glanced back at Christian and smiled. "Your father must have loved your mother very much."

He nodded. "They started as friends, but that friendship turned to love. He gave her that ring on their tenth wedding anniversary. I'll never forget the look on her face. The sheer pleasure in her eyes."

"She was lucky to have his love."

"And I am lucky to have your love."

Her pulse skittered seeing the love and passion in his eyes.

"Are you hungry?" he asked, nipping at her ear.

"Not really."

"Wine?"

"Please."

He walked to the table, filled both glasses and handed one to her.

"I have something for you. I've been wanting to give it to you for days now."

She loved surprises. "What is it?"

He shook his head. "No, I'm going to blindfold you first."

Skeptical, she furrowed her brows. "What are you up to?"

Shrugging, he pulled a black sash from his robe pocket and wrapped it around her head, tying it snugly so she could not see. "Come." He helped her out of her robe, and it fell to her feet as he lifted her. Stepping up onto the bed, he deposited her on the silk sheets. She wriggled, and the smooth silk felt wonderful against her bottom.

"I think I like this game."

"It's about to get better." His voice was as soft as the silk beneath her.

He took her hand, kissed it lightly, then brought it up over her head. Silk wrapped around that wrist, and then the other. Anticipation rippled along her spine. He was tying her to the bed.

Soon her legs were spread, her feet tied securely. Blindfolded she couldn't see where he was, or what he was doing. Excitement built within her as she felt the mattress dip from the weight of his body. "You are so beautiful, my darling wife." He leaned over her and touched his lips to hers.

"And you are wicked."

"No more wicked than you, my dear."

She let out a gasp when something wet was poured over her stomach, pooling in her navel. "Champagne," Christian said a second before his tongue lapped the cool liquid from her heated skin. He knelt between her thighs, hair brushing against her stomach as he nibbled on her skin and licked all the champagne away. Next his tongue laved her nipples, his teeth grazing the tender flesh. He kissed the space between her breasts, then her neck, and her ear. His tongue stroked the ridge of her ear.

Her blood seemed to boil to a white-hot pitch. "Christian," she whispered. She needed him inside of her. "Please…"

"Please, what?" he asked, then smiled against her neck, lips warm and gentle.

He ran his hands down both arms, from hand to shoulders, then down over her breasts, stomach, past her groin, to her thighs, then lower still to her ankles. He proceeded to make his way back up again, stopping this time at the apex of her thighs. His breath came hot against her already-slick folds.

She lifted her hips, and he put a hand on her stomach, holding her down. "Do not move." His voice was firm, but she sensed he smiled.

He touched her with the very tip of his tongue, and she brought her hips to his mouth, seeking more, but he pushed down, keeping her still. His tongue laved her folds, teasing her clit, sucking it. His fingers moved up her body once more, coming close to her sensitive nipples, but never touching them. His tongue caressed her again, his hands spreading her thighs wider, and then he plunged his tongue inside her. She cried out, straining against her bonds.

Christian watched his wife writhe against the bonds that held her as an orgasm overtook her body. Her pink folds glistened with her release and she moaned low in her throat as he kissed her belly. His cock grew harder as she shifted her hips against him, her desire and her frustration clear.

Soon, he would put them both out of their misery.

Lying over her, he ran his cock over her wet slit. She whimpered and he kissed her hard. She kissed him back, her tongue playing with his, circling his, desperate, needy.

His lips made a path down her neck to her breasts where he kissed one nipple then the other. When he pushed the very tip of his cock inside her, she let out a gasp and arched against him, offering herself. He pulled back, giving her just the head of his cock, watching as her breaths came more quickly.

"Christian, please!"

He entered her with a swift thrust, moaning with the pleasure of being inside her hot sheath. He wanted it to last, but he could not wait, especially when her vagina clenched around him. Sweat trickled down his back with the effort to keep himself in check. Alex writhed against the bindings, her wicked words coaxing him on. Desire slithered through him, pulsing within him until he could not hold on. With a cry, he filled her with his seed.

Christian kissed his wife, then gingerly removed the bonds that held her to the bed. She sighed contently and snuggled up to him. She looked at him, her brows furrowed. "What are you looking so pleased about?"

He held her tighter to him, running his fingers over her hip. "I'm thankful that my brother brought you to me."

She grinned. "I'm glad he did, too."

He brushed an auburn curl out of her eyes. "You're the best thing that ever happened to me, do you know that?"

"Well, truth be told, you're the best thing that ever happened to me, too."

Her words filled him with pleasure. If she had not come into his life, he would have gone mad. He knew that now, and realized the sacrifice his brother had made for him. "I guess Devon knew exactly what he was doing when he brought you through time. He knew I would fall in love with you."

"What can I say, he's got good taste."

Christian chuckled. "Yes, he has very good taste, and I will forever be in his debt."

"I don't know if I'd say that too loud. The walls have ears, you know."

Christian gave the room a once over. Certain that his brother had left them alone this evening, he leaned over and gave Alex a kiss. "I love you, Alex."

The corners of her mouth lifted in a soft smile. Her green eyes darkening with passion as she met his gaze. "Why don't you show me again just how much you love me?"

Also by Julia Templeton

ଚ

Dangerous Desire *(also available in print)*
Hometown Hero
Kieran the Black
Now and Forever

About the Author

ଚ

Julia Templeton has written contemporary, historical and time-travel romances for magazines and book publishers and, most recently, romantica for Ellora's Cave Publishing. She also pens novels under the pseudonym Anastasia Black with writing partner and fellow Ellora's Cave author Tracy Cooper-Posey. Aside from her passion for writing, Julia also enjoys reading, listening to music, collecting research books, traveling and spending time with family.

Julia welcomes mail from readers. You can write to her c/o Ellora's Cave Publishing at 1056 Home Ave. Akron, Oh 44310-3502.

TEARS OF AMUN

By Jordan Summers

&

To Si:

The love of my life.

Acknowledgment

ಐ

Many thanks to Mom for her futuristic loan. Dad, my family, and friends for listening to me ramble about writing. And thanks to my critique partner, Chey. I'd also like to thank grandma and Edna who always believed in me. I wish you guys were here to see this moment. And last, but not least, to D.M. for being the best creative writing teacher a high school student could ever ask for.

Chapter One

Egypt, 1925

❧

"Hurry up, Charlotte. Don't dawdle." Frustration pinched Victoria Witherspoon's voice until it squeaked.

"Coming, Mother," Charlotte Witherspoon called out, hastening her step, hoping to avoid her mother's ire.

Charlotte closed her eyes and gritted her teeth, as she pushed down her vexation. This same haunting scenario had been happening every day for as long as she could remember with little variation. Victoria nitpicked her, continuously chipping away at her self-esteem until it lay like rubble upon the ground. Unable to deal with the pain, Charlotte squelched the hurt that twisted her insides. There was no sense dwelling on it.

Balancing her bag in one hand, Charlotte picked up her skirt to step over the fallen rubble that once was the great temple of Karnak. She'd made it a few yards further when her ankle wedged between two rocks and she tripped, the sack flying out of her hands as she tumbled forward. It was at that precise moment that her mother chose to glance back. Charlotte felt heat rise to her face.

"For pity's sake, Charlotte, do pick up your feet like a graceful young lady should." Her mother's hands went to her hips and she shook her head in disapproval. "How many times must I tell you?"

"Sorry, Mother." She pushed herself up off the ground, ignoring the diggers' curious stares. *It's not like I did it on purpose*, Charlotte wanted to say, but didn't dare speak her mind. It would only make matters worse with her mother, the perfect Victoria Witherspoon, who never did anything untoward. Her mother's manners were impeccable, her taste enviable, and she expected nothing less from her only daughter; which made it unfortunate since Charlotte took after her father Henry, a self-professed, slightly clumsy bookworm. Despite being eighteen, a fact her mother refused to acknowledge, Victoria had a way of making Charlotte feel like an inadequate, somewhat dim child.

She brushed her hands on her skirt and picked up the sack she'd dropped. Charlotte opened the bag, taking a quick inventory of the contents. The book she'd borrowed from the lending library in London was still there, along with her brushes. She held her breath as she examined the brushes, looking for any sign of cracks or breaks. She let out a sigh of relief. Thank goodness the brushes were intact. Charlotte didn't want to receive another lecture on carelessness. Assured she hadn't lost anything, she closed the sack and continued on.

Her parents had already slipped into one of the chambers leaving Charlotte standing at the entrance breathing stale air. Their minds were one-track when they were on-site. They probably hadn't even noticed she was missing, not that the oversight was something new. Charlotte was quite used to being considered a nuisance. Instead of allowing her to stay home, curled up with a good book, her mother insisted she be at the dig.

Instead of following, she stepped back into the sunlight, blinking against the glare. Her parents would be in there for the rest of the day and probably into the night, making traces. Charlotte expelled a heavy breath, knowing she should follow them, but unable to bring herself to do so. She was itching to get at the book in her sack.

She spun on her heel and made her way around the ruins to a spot near some newly uncovered stairs. Huge sand piles hugged the sides of the staircase, like a giant hourglass that had been tipped on end, lending itself as the perfect hideaway. Charlotte sat on the highest step, drawing out the book. She cracked open the cover, a musty smell indicative of an old tomb wafted from the pages. Charlotte leaned forward and inhaled deeply, closing her eyes for a second in delight. There were few things on Earth that struck her as close to the soul as a good book.

Methodically she thumbed through the satiny sheets until she'd found her favorite spot. Pictures of the pharaohs gliding across the cool waters of the Nile came to life before her eyes, their bronze skin glowing against the white linen of their embroidered kilts. Charlotte's gaze caressed the figures, focusing on one man in particular. His chest was bare and unusually broad for an Egyptian. His arms appeared strong, bulging with muscles. The man's kohl-lined black eyes seemed to penetrate the very pages, demanding her attention, drawing her nearer.

Charlotte ran her fingers over the image. Goosebumps immediately rose on her arms. She knew she was being silly but for some reason couldn't bring herself to stop returning to him over and over. She'd loved this man since she was fifteen years old, if it were even possible to fall in love with an image.

She'd even gone so far as to imagine their life together, what it would feel like if he held her in his arms, pressed his lips to hers. Would his lips be firm or soft? Wet or dry? Charlotte knew if she'd mentioned her infatuation with the picture, her mother would remind her that she needed to get her head out of the clouds and meet a nice young man to settle down with.

That would take all your fanciful notions away tout suite. Really Charlotte, sometimes I wonder where your head is…

Her mother didn't need to be standing in front of her for Charlotte to be able to hear her admonishing voice clearly in her mind. Charlotte harrumphed. She knew there wasn't much chance of meeting someone suitable on a dig site in Thebes. All the eligible men she'd considered taking a shine to had been far too wrapped up in trying to make the next big discovery to even notice she was there. Not that Charlotte cared. She wasn't interested in anyone but the commanding man in the picture.

"If only you were real," she muttered under her breath, running her fingers over his still form.

She glanced down at the byline under the papyrus. The Egyptologist who'd written the book had believed the figure in the depiction was King Amasis, but had put a side note at the bottom explaining his lack of evidence and all around uncertainty.

"Little help you are," she spoke to the picture, laughing.

Ever since Charlotte had learned his name, she'd had a vague sense of dèjá vu, but couldn't understand why. Once again she could almost hear her mother *tsking* in disapproval. Charlotte closed the book and put it aside, picking up her brush in its stead. It was time to get to work. At least if her mother wandered by she'd appear to be busy. The air settled around her, hot and oppressive, as she dusted away debris from the half-exposed step with a swish from the brush in her hand.

It had been three years since Mr. Carter and Lord Carnarvon had uncovered the find of the century, Tutankhamen's tomb. She'd been relegated to this small area of Karnak along with her parents, lesser known explorers who strived for one thing only: the preservation of Egyptian history. While the *true* Egyptologists were free to delve into the Valley of the Kings.

She stopped, laying the brush down at her side. It wasn't fair. Her parents had been here just as long as Howard Carter, if not longer. They should have been the ones to stumble upon such a great find as Tutankhamen.

Charlotte sighed and went back to work, toiling deeper into the sand, pushing thoughts of treasure from her mind. She had made three more swipes when her hand struck something hard beneath the sand. Her breath seized and her heart thudded wildly in her chest. Her vision narrowed to where her hand lay still against the hidden item. With trembling fingers, Charlotte carefully cleared the area. The sounds around her muted as she uncovered a small wooden case.

At first glance, it didn't look like much. Perhaps a toy left behind by a child, or a worker's tool kit, long buried in the unforgiving sand. Upon closer inspection, Charlotte changed her mind. She leaned back and glanced around the pile of sand to make sure none of the nearby diggers had observed her making the discovery. All eyes were upon the tasks at hand as they rhythmically worked with picks and shovels.

Charlotte stood, wiping the dust from her hands. She slid the item, along with her brush and book into her sack and made her way to the sacred lake of Karnak. In the late morning the area tended to be deserted. She'd be able to examine her find before taking it to her parents. Perhaps it would be good enough to garner them the recognition they deserved and get them moved to a more prestigious area to dig. Surely if Charlotte accomplished that, her mother would finally see her worth and begin to love her. She sighed. But first she needed to confirm its authenticity or her mother would never let her live it down.

Walking over the fallen stones, Charlotte rounded the columns along the path, her heels clattering over the rocks. She stared at the ruins for a moment, wishing it were possible to see the temple at Karnak in its full glory. The sun, golden in the sky, shined brightly on the water ahead, twinkling and radiant. It was the perfect spot to uncover her treasure. Charlotte glanced at the glass-like surface, shielding her eyes, so that she wouldn't misstep. The area was empty, except for an occasional goose or two that called the Nile valley home. She found a cleared spot near the water's edge and sat.

Sweat trickled down her neck and under her white blouse. Her eyes once again sought the promise of cooling water. The still liquid, tempting in its calmness, called out to her. Charlotte stamped her foot. She couldn't go swimming in the sacred lake. It was forbidden. Besides, it was probably full of crocodiles.

She removed a handkerchief from her sleeve and dabbed at her forehead. The white linen came away with a smudge of dirt across it. Charlotte humphed. Nothing stayed clean in the middle of the desert. She tucked the now soiled linen back up her sleeve and removed the wooden box and her brush from the sack.

The box was no larger than a thin loaf of bread. She gently blew away the sand covering it. The cartouches were well worn, but still clearly visible in their gold inlay. Charlotte stared in wonder, turning the box this way and that, studying the craftsmanship. The wood felt rough against her fingertips from the harsh treatment of the sand.

She looked for an opening. There didn't appear to be one. It certainly hadn't belonged to a commoner. Had a thief dropped it while trying to make his escape? It wouldn't be the first time artifacts had been found discarded in the sand like rubbish. She shook her head in disgust.

She picked up her brush and proceeded to clear away the last remnants of sand until she was able to read the inscription. Charlotte's eye's widened as the words on the box came to life in her mind.

Through the sands of time

By the pharaoh's breath

When the waters rise to highest depth

Then the veils will thin

For two worlds to see

A fated love that must once again be

He who gazes upon the one wearing the Tears of Amun

Shall go on to rule the kingdoms of Egypt

Charlotte almost dropped the box as she read the last words. It didn't sound like a curse, but it definitely sounded ominous. She set the box down, taking a moment to catch her breath. Who had owned this and what were the Tears of Amun? She'd never heard of them, even though her parents had taken care to teach her about all of the legends and pharaohs that existed in ancient times.

They'd pounded everything Egyptian into her head, until she could read and write Hieratic, Demotic, and Hieroglyphs. Charlotte could also speak Arabic, Coptic, and even a little Ancient Egyptian; although she was unsure whether her pronunciations on the latter two were correct, since they had been virtually extinct for over a thousand years. She picked the box up again to examine it further, the words inscribed on top floating through her mind like an apparition. Its presence, a ghostly voice from the past, spoke to her.

Her mother and father had warned her about curses, although they didn't believe in them personally. Charlotte wasn't so sure. Howard Carter had lost several men who'd been there to open Tutankhamen's tomb. Whispers of a curse had spread like wildfire throughout the campsites. Charlotte shivered at the thought.

She heard a splash as something hit the water. Charlotte jumped, her hand automatically flying to her heart, before spotting the culprit. A duck paddled around the center of the lake, unconcerned with her presence, quacking away. She laughed, the nervous sound strained to her own ears. Why was she so jumpy? It wasn't like she'd done anything wrong.

Sweat was now pouring off her. She told herself she'd just go to the water's edge to wet her handkerchief, then come right back. Charlotte went to stand the box on end, when a latch she hadn't noticed before slid free. A golden necklace dropped out on the ground with a clunk. Her breath caught. The sun sparkled off the precious metal, glimmering red on the stones inlayed in the gold. They were teardrop shaped and as crimson as blood. Charlotte gasped—rubies. She ran her fingers over the gems.

The Tears of Amun…

Charlotte heard footsteps and immediately grabbed the necklace, slipping it over her head before someone could spot her. Hanif, one of the workers, stepped from behind a column, his slight body drenched in sweat. She waved to him. Hanif smiled back, white teeth flashing against bronze skin. The man turned silently, as if realizing he'd intruded on her space. Once again she was left alone with her thoughts and her precious treasure.

Charlotte's head was spinning. The gold and jewels around her neck were heavy, weighted. The gold heated her skin, eclipsing the warmth of the day. Lightheaded, she made her way to the water, pulling a square of soft linen from her sleeve. She knelt down near the edge to dip her handkerchief in the liquid. Unable to reach, Charlotte inched closer. The rock near the shore crumbled, toppling her headfirst into Karnak's sacred lake. The air was knocked from Charlotte's lungs as she hit the water.

The lake was hot, stagnant from lack of current. As she struggled to break the surface, Charlotte felt as if a thousand hands were tugging her from below, preventing her from gasping much needed air. She opened her eyes. Her movements slowed as she watched the light from the sun fade and reappear over and over again. Surely her mind was playing tricks on her due to lack of oxygen. She blinked.

Fear surged through her, giving her an added boost of adrenaline. Charlotte broke the surface, sputtering and coughing, trying to rid her lungs of Nile water. Reaching out with both hands she grasped the rough stones near the water's edge. Her hat was gone, leaving her curly brown hair plastered to her back. Her clothes hugged her like a second skin. She brushed a hand over her face, ridding her eyes of water. Geese honked overhead as they flew by.

Charlotte blinked again as she pulled herself out of the lake enough to sit on the stone edge. She scanned the area, a frown upon her face. Once again she wiped at her eyes while her mind struggled to decipher what she was seeing. The columns in Karnak were aligned with intricate carvings at the base, not crumbling and worn. She stood to get a better view. The stones that she'd carefully maneuvered around to get to the sacred lake were smoothed into level walkways. A wall rose up in the distance marking the entrance into the temple area. Charlotte reached over and pinched her hand.

"Ouch!"

Her flesh turned an angry pink upon contact. Well at least she knew she wasn't dreaming. Was it possible that she'd drowned? She glanced out at the lake and saw craft upon the

Nile in the distance. They didn't look like the normal boats used by modern Egyptians. They appeared to be longer, thinner. Dark-haired people dressed in white linen stood at the ends of the vessels steering them through the black water.

"Oh my…this can't be…it isn't possible," Charlotte muttered to herself. "I must have hit my head on the bottom." She closed her eyes, resting her head in her hands. Perhaps if she sat here long enough the world would return to normal. "It's only a dream, a bad, bad dream." A cough coming from behind one of the nearby columns jolted Charlotte back to reality.

"Hanif, is that you?" she called out.

There was no answer.

"Hanif, I've had a terribly bad day. Please show yourself." Her voice quivered.

A brown hand appeared to the side of the column. Charlotte released the breath she hadn't known she'd been holding and waited for Hanif to appear. Instead, the most striking man Charlotte had ever seen stepped from behind the column. He wore a white linen kilt with embroidery at the top around his slim hips. The material hung down to his knees, leaving his well-developed calves exposed. His dark eyes, slightly slanted, were lined with kohl, like the ancient Egyptians had been depicted in carvings for thousands of years.

Charlotte frowned. He looked familiar.

His chest was wide and heavily muscled. Gold bracelets with blue scarabs crowning the tops bound his wrists. A gold necklace bearing the shape of three flies circled his throat. Hair of the blackest night hung to his shoulders and had been ornately braided. Charlotte instantly recognized the necklace as a sign of bravery. Why was he wearing it? And who was he?

His face was a work of art, sculpted with high cheekbones and full lips, squaring into a firm chin. His black eyes were heated, intense. His gaze was locked on the front of her shirt. Charlotte watched the rise and fall of his chest, the rhythm mesmerizing, as his fire took hold of her. She glanced down to see what was held him so captivated.

The white of her shirt had turned transparent from the water. The Tears of Amun were clearly visible through the garment, along with her rosy nipples, which had taken that moment to bead under his close scrutiny. Charlotte sucked in a surprised breath and covered her breasts with her hands.

For a moment more, his gaze lingered before returning to her face. When his eyes met hers, he smiled. The simple act melted her insides.

He was the man from her book.

The same man she'd spent countless hours gaping at like a schoolgirl suffering from her first crush—except he was real. It wasn't possible, *was it*? Had she wished so hard, he'd come true?

Charlotte felt heat start at her toes, rise along her legs, over her knees, gravitating to the apex between her ample thighs. If he could do that with just a look, what would it feel like if he touched her? The traitorous thought entered her mind, sending warmth flaring to her face. She knew without the aid of a mirror, she was blushing.

Her dream man stepped forward. Charlotte hadn't noticed the harpoon in his other hand. She glanced over her shoulder at the water. There was nowhere for her to escape. Her eyes once again found his. He paused, frowning as if reading her thoughts. Charlotte forced herself to smile, willing herself to keep calm until she could figure out what was going on.

Of course, why panic over the fact that my fantasy man has come to life from the pages of a book? It happens all the time. Yes, and Mother thinks I'm the perfect daughter.

The man continued on slowly, making his way toward her until they were standing but a yard apart. The detail of his clothing was unmistakable. Charlotte had never seen anything like it with the exception of Howard Carter's finds and the book she'd borrowed from the library. She glanced to the ground where she'd left her sack before falling into the lake, but it was gone.

Charlotte looked back at the man before her. A shift of the wind brought his spicy scent to her. Shock and awareness slammed into her body. Her knees weakened as she inhaled deeply. Her senses came alive, zeroing in on the man before her. The juncture between her thighs started to throb. Her nipples beaded painfully. It was as if his mere presence jolted her awake from a deep, deep sleep. Charlotte fought the urge to move closer so she could inhale more of his essence. Touch his bronze skin. He was even more handsome than she'd imagined. The picture did not do justice to this striking figure.

What was she saying?

In all likelihood this man simply resembled the man in the picture. He couldn't possibly be him. That man's name was Amasis and he'd lived over two thousand years ago. Charlotte felt the back of her head, her fingers tangling in her wet locks. There had to be an injury somewhere. She gave up after a moment, unable to locate a wound.

If she wasn't hurt, then she needed to figure out where he had gotten all of the items on his body. She needed to authenticate what she was seeing, and then inform her parents of the find. Charlotte was sure her mother would have a thing or two to say about her appearance, but it couldn't be helped. After all, she hadn't planned to take a swim in the sacred lake. It was an accident, like all the other times…

She held out her hand. "My name is Miss Charlotte Witherspoon."

The man looked at her hand and then back to her face. When he made no move, Charlotte clasped his hand. His large palm enveloped hers, sending delicious tingles racing up her arm. His eyes widened but he didn't pull away.

"It's nice to meet you," she prompted, before quickly releasing him.

Still nothing.

She blew out a ragged breath and ran her hand through her hair. Charlotte wasn't sure why the man wasn't speaking. *Fantasies don't talk,* the little voice in her head chided. She dismissed the thought with a wave of her hand. She needed to focus, but it was difficult with the resemblance to the picture being so uncanny. Perhaps he refused to talk because he thought she'd turn him in for theft. Charlotte glanced at his necklace. For something over two thousand years old, it showed remarkably little wear and tear. In fact, it looked almost new, along with the temple's reconstruction, which was impossible.

"What is your name?" she asked in her best Egyptian tongue, the words stumbling from her lips.

His brows furrowed and then rose as he finally comprehended. "My name is Ahmose." He pressed a large hand to his wide chest.

"Ahmose," she repeated, letting the name play across her mouth. Charlotte tried to ignore the way his taut skin was stretched across a canvas of hard muscle. "I like it." She smiled. At least that answered the question at the back of her mind. He wasn't the man in the picture. His name wasn't common in Egypt, but that didn't necessarily mean anything. Familiar, yet not. She brushed it away, deciding to examine it later.

Charlotte placed a hand over her breast, her erect nipple stabbing her palm. Surprised by her body's strange reaction to the man's nearness, she gulped and forged on, praying he hadn't noticed. "I'm Charlotte Witherspoon."

He stared at her for a moment, his gaze caressing the rigid crests, as if they were still visible. Her skin prickled. Then once again he sought her eyes, his lips now pursing to try and mimic what she'd said. *Well so much for him not noticing…*She flushed as she repeated her name.

"Ch-aaarleete," he said attempting to imitate the sound she'd created.

Charlotte nodded encouragingly. "Charlotte."

"Ch-charlotte," he said again.

"Yes." She smiled.

Charlotte glanced over his shoulder at the temple of Karnak. Why wasn't it in ruin? As the question ran through her mind again, her head began to swim. The temple was complete, not a stone out of place. There were no ruins in sight. She'd really thought her fall in the water had affected her perception, but since Karnak was still whole, Charlotte was beginning to get worried.

Several men rushed toward their location, weapons drawn, dressed exactly like Ahmose.

This wasn't conceivable. There was no way this could be happening. The man standing before her wasn't her dream. She'd already confirmed that. Charlotte shook her head in denial. She was not back in ancient Egypt, it wasn't possible. She couldn't be seeing what she was seeing.

Charlotte's gaze locked onto his and she swayed. The man grabbed her. The warmth from his palms penetrated her skin just as her world faded into darkness.

Chapter Two

෨

Charlotte's lids fluttered as she willed herself to open her eyes. No longer hot, she felt comfortable for the first time in a while. She stretched, trying to recall what she'd been doing earlier. She'd found a necklace while sitting beside the sacred lake at Karnak. She'd also been talking to the most beautiful man she'd ever laid eyes on, and then everything went black.

Charlotte's eyes flew open. Had he struck her? No, she didn't think so, her head bore no pain. She glanced around at her surroundings. She was inside of a chamber of some kind. Torches protruded from the sienna-colored walls, lighting the area. A ceremonial-looking axe hung between two torches, its gold glittering in the firelight. Shifting, Charlotte looked down at her side. She'd been placed upon a bed constructed of mud brick that appeared to be layered in reed mats and then covered with thin linen. The material was soft against her skin. The odor of frankincense wafted in the air, its spicy aroma soothing.

She turned over, allowing the material to slip down her shoulder and over the fine hairs on her arm like a sensuous caress. A slight scrape over her nipples drew her attention down. Her eyes widened. Her clothes were gone. She was lying in the bed naked with the Tears of Amun around her neck. The rouged pink of her nipples poked out over the top of the covers.

Confused, Charlotte pulled the linen close and glanced around the room again, ensuring she was alone. Had the man resembling the picture undressed her? What had it felt like to have his large hands on her body? Were his palms rough or smooth? Had he taken his time lingering over her breasts, perhaps stroking the tuft of hair between her legs? She squeezed her thighs together to halt the ache that had begun. Charlotte tried to muster outrage, but could only manage insatiable curiosity.

She flopped down on her back and stared up at the ceiling while she tried to make sense of the situation. Leaves had been intricately painted on the mud brick ceiling giving her the sensation of being out-of-doors. The walls were smooth and appeared to be thick, lending to the coolness in the room, the firelight giving them a golden glow. The details were familiar to her, but different. The only time she'd seen anything similar was on a dig and no one in those sites had lived in the dwellings for over two thousand years. It just didn't make sense.

Footsteps down the hall were her only warning a moment before Ahmose appeared in the doorway. Charlotte whipped the covers up to her chin, suddenly feeling vulnerable and small in his presence. He looked as handsome as before with his brown sun-kissed complexion and brilliant smile. His skin had been oiled, carrying the aroma of myrrh.

He opened his mouth and began to speak. The slight difference in dialect compared to what she'd studied had her scrambling to keep up. In over a thousand years no one had heard ancient Egyptian spoken aloud. And no matter what her mind was telling her, Charlotte knew beyond a doubt that was exactly what he was speaking.

For a few seconds she just stared in wonder, listening to the words roll seductively off his tongue, her fantasy come to life. From her earliest memory, Charlotte had been surrounded by Egypt and the digs. Her parents had brought her on her first excavation when she'd been barely able to toddle. They'd filled her head with tales of the ancient kingdom and of the great rulers and cities that had once existed. It had been Charlotte's fondest wish at the time to be able to see the cities in all their glory, exactly how her parents had described. And from the looks of things, it had come true.

"Be careful what you wish for, Charlotte Witherspoon," she murmured under her breath.

The man arched his brow.

"W-where a-am I?" Charlotte struggled to speak his language, enunciating every word to make sure she was understood. Her lips puckered as she twisted her tongue around the dialect. Having never heard ancient Egyptian spoken it was difficult, to say the very least.

He looked around the room. "You are in my home."

"But where exactly is that?" She glanced at the walls, then back to his face, all the while keeping herself covered.

"The great capital city of Egypt—Thebes." Ahmose's hands moved to his hips and his chest seemed to puff out at the proclamation.

Charlotte's brows knitted. Thebes wasn't the capital of Egypt, but she wasn't about to tell Ahmose that, especially with everything else going on. She didn't want to know, but she had to ask.

"Who is the leader of this land?" Charlotte's fingers gripped the material at her throat until her knuckles turned white.

"The great King Kamose, my brother," he replied, as if she were dense.

Charlotte's mind refused to function. The pharaoh Kamose ruled in the Second Intermediate Period followed by Ahmose the first, who heralded in the New Kingdom. Charlotte's eyes locked with his. She couldn't seem to catch her breath.

This was Prince Ahmose, the man who would be King. Or as the Greeks called him, Amasis, the very man from the picture in her book.

Charlotte brought a hand to her head, trying to stop the wave of dizziness threatening to overtake her.

"You wear the Tears of Amun." He pointed to the spot beneath the linen where the jewels poked through.

She glanced down at the necklace beneath the covers.

"Do you know what this means?" he asked, as he crossed his arms over his chest.

Charlotte wasn't absolutely positive, but from the inscription she had a pretty good idea. Perhaps it had been a curse after all, considering she'd been catapulted through time. With speed she hadn't anticipated, Ahmose closed the distance between them, snatching the cover down while she was lost in thought.

"Wait one minute." She tried to grab the cover back, but his grip was too firm.

He slid his hand beneath the necklace. "It means that whoever gazes upon the Tears of Amun shall rule all the kingdoms of Egypt, with the wearer by his side."

Charlotte's eyes practically bugged out of her head. "It didn't say that," she whispered, distracted by the heat of his hands.

"The last part I added myself," he practically purred. "I care not, whence you came. Nor that you speak my tongue strangely. Only that you are here now to become my qefent."

Charlotte couldn't seem to focus. She must have misunderstood him. Had he just told her he wanted her cunt? She blinked, retracing his words, before remembering the other meaning of the word. Surely he didn't expect her to…to become his qefent—his wife?

His gaze heated as it latched onto her nipples. Charlotte's body responded, despite her shock and the need to protect her modesty. With his free hand, Ahmose dropped the necklace and reached out slowly, giving her plenty of time to move away, until his fingertips made contact with her jutting flesh.

Charlotte gasped, then sucked in a surprised breath at her body's response to the warmth radiating from his hands. No one had ever touched her so intimately. Growing up on a dig site had kept her fairly isolated. Had it not been for reading Casanova's "The Story of My Life" she would be completely ignorant. As it was, she'd only managed to experience the sensation of kissing a couple of years ago on her sixteenth birthday. Luckily for her, Victoria had been too preoccupied to know of either event.

Ahmose fondled her nipples, drawing her back from her musings. Charlotte knew she should slap his hand away. But her flesh had begun to tingle, feeling as if a fire had been lit beneath its surface. Besides, being in another time period, things like this held no consequence, *did they*?

He circled her nipple with the pad of his thumb, until it was standing at attention, begging for more. Charlotte's breasts ached and began to throb. She burned for him. He pinched her nipple gently and she moaned. Without thought Charlotte leaned into his hand, seeking his scorching touch. His eyes were locked on her face as if gauging her reaction. She flushed from head to toe.

No matter how hard she tried to fight herself, Charlotte couldn't seem to utter the words to make him stop. She'd dreamt of this moment with him for years. Everything felt so new and exciting, yet so right as if they'd done this a thousand times before. Was it wrong to want to experience something so beautiful with the man she'd loved since the age of fifteen? Her mind refused to think so.

Charlotte stared at his mouth, wanting more than anything to feel his lips upon hers. What he was doing with his hands was driving her insane. She couldn't seem to think clearly, focusing solely on his insistent massage. The ache between her legs had grown to an inferno and she had no idea how to assuage it.

He plucked at her nipple and Charlotte's lips parted. Ahmose didn't hesitate. He swooped down and captured her mouth, drawing out a teasing kiss. Charlotte's body fired off every nerve at once. She couldn't breathe. Her heart was pounding in her chest loud enough to make her believe Ahmose could probably hear it. He tasted of spice and honey, blended nicely with all that was male. She found him utterly intoxicating and was drowning in his embrace.

It wasn't enough. Suddenly there were too many covers on her body. She pushed at them, until he let them drop from his hands and onto the floor. Charlotte sat up to meet his lips. The second her naked body made contact with his muscled chest, her world tilted.

She was on fire. Skin on skin, their bodies slid together as if they were meant to be. He deepened the kiss, tentatively dipping his tongue, then plunging in once she didn't recoil. Charlotte's fingers reached out and grasped his forearms to keep herself from being pulled over the edge into the abyss. He increased the pressure on her mouth, dominating. A growl escaped from the back of his throat, as Ahmose's hands slid over her breasts and around her waist until he could cup her bottom. Charlotte gasped against his mouth, her fingers digging into his skin. They merged once more, the kiss turning fierce.

Within seconds she was being gently guided back onto the bed. Once she was lying flat, he broke the kiss and stepped back to remove his embroidered linen kilt. It fell away from his body. Charlotte's eyes locked onto the rising cock nestled within a bed of crisp ebony curls between his legs. It was as thick as her wrist.

Heat had gathered and pooled between her legs along with moisture. Her lungs heaved in air as he slowly approached the bed and lay down beside her. Every rule she'd been taught about the proper etiquette for young ladies flew out the window when Ahmose touched her nipple again.

His mouth came down on her breast and her nipple sprang to life like a long dormant flower. He suckled and licked, teasing the bud into bloom. Charlotte cried out, shifting her hips in invitation. Her senses were in overload and she couldn't seem to take in everything that was happening. She wanted this man more than she'd ever wanted anything, yet she didn't really know him, only knew *of* him. Ahmose finally took a breath, giving Charlotte a moment to gather her addled wits.

"We shouldn't be doing this," she gasped, as he ran a finger along her arm. "We don't really know each other."

"We have a lifetime to get to know each other." His eyes were intent as he focused on her face. "Our destiny was written long ago. It cannot be avoided or ignored." His deep voice was raspy as he spoke.

Charlotte tried to concentrate on his words, so she could come up with a viable argument. This was wrong. They were wrong. She wasn't meant to be here, *was she*? She shouldn't even be contemplating having sex with this man. *It's all you've ever dreamed of,* the random thought entered her mind. Eventually she'd have to return to her own time. Her parents were probably worried sick. *If they even notice you're gone*, the little voice inside her head whispered. *Why not enjoy the time you have here?*

Even as the thoughts swept across her mind, Ahmose's hands were beginning to do strange things to her ability to reason. He stroked lightly over her skin, leaving gooseflesh behind. His breathing had deepened until it matched hers, calming, reassuring. Charlotte's gaze found his black eyes. They were like molten liquid, shimmering, fiery and scalding in intensity. The temperature in the room seemed to rise within seconds. Charlotte felt feverish, needy. Her pussy ached.

Ahmose smiled in understanding then dipped his head down to the other breast that had been neglected earlier. Charlotte's lids dropped, colors exploded behind them. All thoughts of refuting him and returning to her own time left her head. Her body was his for the taking. She let him explore freely.

Ahmose examined all of Charlotte's hidden peaks and valleys. He couldn't seem to get enough of the fair vision that had appeared out of the sacred lake. He knew better than to question the gods on their wisdom. She arrived bearing the Tears of Amun, which was all he needed to know. He would follow his destiny as was foretold in the stars and bring the kingdoms of Egypt together once again.

He caressed her nipples, the rosy skin as soft as the petals on a flower. His fingers trembled as he lingered over the soft curves of her full breasts. Ahmose dipped between the valley, trailing his finger down toward her navel. He circled the sensitive area several times, before following the same route with his mouth. Her breath seized as he placed tiny kisses across her skin. Ahmose sensed her inexperience and slowed his exploration. He wanted to take the time to cherish this gift, pay homage to her beauty. Praise be to the gods.

Charlotte's full hips bucked as he ran his hand along her leg, scraping his nails over her thigh. She peeked out from beneath her lids, following his exploration. Ahmose marveled at the contrast between the white of her skin against the brown of his hands. The oil from his body added to the glide as he made his way over her flesh, intoxicated.

Ahmose slid down until his head was situated above her mon. The sweet aroma of Charlotte's arousal wafted in the air, mingling with the myrrh on his skin and the frankincense. He inhaled deeply, dipping one finger into her wetness. She gasped. Her eyes flew open, locking on his seeking fingers.

"Such beauty," he murmured low. "You are fairer than the flowers growing along the Nile." He slipped the finger into his mouth. "And far sweeter."

Charlotte blushed.

Ahmose swiped his finger again, this time connecting with the bundle of nerves hidden beneath her folds.

Charlotte thought she was going to come off the bed, her body was responding in ways she was unfamiliar with. She had the overwhelming urge to hang on to something, just so she wouldn't fly apart into a million pieces. Ahmose dipped his head and laved the same spot he'd just touched.

Charlotte gasped. "What are you doing?"

"Loving you…"

Her world narrowed to his insistent mouth. Nothing else mattered or existed. Ahmose shifted again until his body was positioned between her thighs. He dove between her legs, lapping and thrusting at her clitoris with his tongue.

Charlotte could feel tension building inside her, winding tighter and tighter, as if drawing her near a razor's edge. Her hips were moving of their own volition, trying to match his probing. Charlotte grasped his head, her fingers sinking into his ebony hair as her pussy pulsed with need. It seemed to be all the encouragement Ahmose required. He became frenzied, feeding at her woman's center, plunging into her drenched channel.

The blood was pounding so loudly in her ears Charlotte could hardly hear. "Please," she begged, not at all sure exactly what she was asking for. She closed her eyes against the sensation. Her hips thrust against his mouth, wanting, needing, and desiring something more.

Ahmose sucked her clitoris between his teeth and purred, vibrating the sensitive flesh, until a dam seemed to burst inside of her. Charlotte cried out again as she slipped over the precipice and into the unknown below. Her body tingled from head to toe, her legs shaking around his head. Charlotte couldn't seem to stop twitching, as contraction after contraction of pleasure rocked through her.

When Charlotte finally opened her eyes and could focus, she glanced up into the smiling face of Ahmose. His grin said it all. He was more than pleased with what he'd done to her. He positively glowed. The second Charlotte recalled exactly what she'd let him do, her gaze dropped. She didn't think she'd ever be able to look Ahmose in the face again. He'd kissed her and she'd turned positively wanton in his arms, thrusting her sex in his face like a dog in heat. What must he think of her?

As if reading her thoughts, Ahmose shifted, until his hips were cradled within her own. Charlotte's gaze flew up, meeting his eyes. She could feel the hard evidence of his arousal, digging into her soft belly. He held her captive as if willing her to recognize the woman she was about to become.

"I'm not so sure I can do this," she whispered.

He smiled again, his cock bucking against her skin. "We have been made for this since the beginning of time, my precious jewel. Trust in what is to be."

Ahmose shifted his hips until his cock lay poised at her entrance. It took every fiber of his being to keep from thrusting forward and taking what was rightfully his. He wanted

Charlotte to go on this journey with him. He slipped his hand between their bodies and began to rub the crown of his shaft over her slick folds. She sucked in a breath, then bit her lip. Ahmose allowed the head to slide into her entrance—it was like heaven, tight, hot, and oh so pleasurable. Charlotte's eyes widened in surprise, but did not show fear. That fact made him prouder than it should have.

"This will hurt but for a moment, my love," he murmured against her cheek as he placed kisses upon her face.

Ahmose slipped his cock in a few more inches, until he encountered her thin barrier. Her velvet channel was molten as it gripped his length, drawing him deeper inside her sheath. There was no easy way to aid this first joining. Ahmose leaned over, latching onto her nipple with his mouth, and thrust forward at the same time. A pain-filled gasp escaped from Charlotte's lips, but he continued to embrace her, lapping at her nipple soothingly. He held his body completely still, the muscles in his back and buttocks straining against the urge to seek his completion.

Charlotte couldn't breath. The pain…the pain she'd felt moments ago was fading and turning into something else. She felt full, stuffed, and unable to move. Ahmose was in her, surrounding, dominating her with his presence. Before this, she hadn't thought their joining possible, but now her body was adjusting, accepting, and welcoming his cock as if it belonged. He slowly released her nipple. Just when Charlotte thought the sensations would cease, he moved, a gentle thrust at first, testing her. She gasped, but instead of pain she felt only pleasure.

Her nipples beaded against the scrape of his hairless chest as he rose up to support himself with his elbows. The small movement brought him deeper inside of her, nudging her womb. Her channel flooded once again, accommodating his size.

"Are you all right?" he asked, little lines creasing his face while concern marred his brow.

"I'm fine. It feels…"

He thrust again. And passion exploded inside of her.

"Wonderful." The word came out on a sigh.

He smiled down at her as he picked up speed. His cock plunged deeper, his rhythm picking her up and carrying her along on a wave of desire. He rocked sideways, massaging a spot inside of her that was almost as sensitive as the little nub on the outside. Charlotte allowed herself to fall into the feeling. Ahmose's hips bucked and surged, pistoning faster and faster. Charlotte's lids started to fall.

"No," he cried. "I want you to look at me when you come again." The muscles in his neck strained. "I want you to know who will be your king."

Charlotte opened her mouth. She wasn't sure if she was about to protest or concur. Ahmose took that moment to dip his tongue inside, circling and twisting with her own. The now familiar throbbing sensation started low in her belly. Charlotte's grip tightened. Ahmose drove deep again and again, centering his effort at her very core. It was all that was needed to hurl Charlotte into another orgasm. She pulled back and screamed, all of her muscles tensing at once, her pussy milking his cock.

The second her sheath grabbed him it was over for Ahmose, and his seed began to spill from his body. Her unrestrained response sent him into oblivion. His hips continued to move as the last of his essence was emptied into the center that would soon hold new life. This wonderful gift from the gods was his, all his and he had no intention of ever letting her go.

Before he'd given it another thought, Ahmose decided they would wed before the celebration of the Opet. Charlotte would become his princess and then later his queen.

Charlotte was seeing stars across the handsome face above her. He was everything she'd ever imagined in a lover and more. His passion had been limitless. They were still joined, but the fact no longer held embarrassment, only joy. Her heart swelled as she felt him throb inside her.

This man, this prince, had wanted her, Charlotte Witherspoon, the woman who'd fallen in love with a picture, when he could have had anyone in the kingdom. The thought was empowering. She reached up and moved a satiny braid of his hair over his shoulder, so that she could see his face clearly. He was grinning down at her, possession burning in his eyes.

A loving curve touched Charlotte's lips.

"What brings you joy?" His smile reached his eyes.

She ran her finger along his jaw. "I was just thinking how lucky I am to have found someone like you to be my first lover."

His expression darkened, storm clouds filling his eyes.

Charlotte dropped her hand away. "Did I say something wrong?"

"You shall have no other lovers from this day forth. You have given yourself to me. I have planted my seed. It is done." He slipped from inside her and slid off her body.

Suddenly Charlotte felt cold, empty. She frowned as she tried to think about his words. "You can't expect me to stay here. I don't belong in this t—"

"I shall hear no more of this." He fastened his kilt in haste. "You are to become my wife."

"Wife!" Charlotte sat up, scrambling for the covers at the same time. "I can't become your wife. I have to get back."

For a moment an expression of confusion crossed Ahmose's face, then just as quickly it cleared. "I will offer the proper gifts, ones fitting for a soon to be queen. Tell me what land I must send them to and it shall be done."

"Queen? Land?" Charlotte was struggling to keep up—first his wife, then his queen? The pieces of the inscription fell into place like an iron latch. "Ahmose, there's been a terrible mistake. The Tears of Amun aren't mine."

He stared, aghast. "You stole them from their rightful owner?"

Charlotte's mouth dropped open. "I would never."

Relief flooded his features. "Then it is settled. We wed in a few days, just in time to join the Opet festival."

She simply stared, unsure of what to say next.

"I will return with some clothing, since your old garments were…unsuitable." Ahmose slipped from the room before she could respond.

Charlotte watched his retreating back until he disappeared around a corner. She had to explain, try to convince him to call the wedding off. Her heart sank. It would do no good falling in love with the man, when in the end she'd have to leave him.

Who was she trying to kid? She'd fallen for Ahmose years ago when his name had been Amasis and he'd only been a picture on a page. The thought of never seeing him again bothered Charlotte more than she cared to admit. After today, how was she going to live without him? The thought was too painful to contemplate.

Chapter Three

🔊

Charlotte lay on the bed, sated, awaiting Ahmose's return. As much as she liked being here with him and experiencing the joys of lovemaking, she had to find a way out of his time and back into her own. If there was a way in, there had to be a way out. Besides, if she ended up staying, history could be irrevocably altered. The question was…how to get back.

She was playing with the gold around her neck when Ahmose returned. He brought her delicate linen, much like what he wore, and carried a wooden chest, laminated in precious gems and mother of pearl, which he proceeded to open. Charlotte almost fell off the bed when she saw the jewels and mass of wealth he displayed. Only in Tutankhamen's tomb did gold like this exist. Her heart thudded as he picked up a ring of gold. Charlotte stared as he slid the ring onto her finger. Tears sprang to her eyes as she realized no matter how much she wanted this, it could never be.

"If you do not like this one, I can get you another." He hesitated, then began to dig through the jewelry.

She swiped at the tears with the back of her hand, then reached to still his movements. "It isn't that. The ring is lovely."

"Then why the tears?" He ran the pad of his thumb over her cheek, wiping away the moisture.

"I'm a little overwhelmed." She shrugged. "I'm a long way from home and not sure how to get back."

He smiled. "Egypt has some of the finest trackers in the land. I'm sure they will find your home, if that is your wish."

Charlotte laughed. She doubted very much if anyone here would be able to find her home. Ahmose reached back in the chest and was once again looking through various items. He picked up two ruby earrings and grinned as he held one up to the side of her face.

"Perfect. They match the Tears of Amun and the fire that lights your eyes."

Charlotte brought his hand to her mouth. She placed a chaste kiss upon his knuckles, before allowing him to hang the earrings from her ears. Ahmose helped her get dressed, showing Charlotte how to tie the linen about her. By the time he'd finished she felt like a true Egyptian princess. He slipped sandals onto her feet and then led her out of the room.

They walked down a narrow corridor into a courtyard. A tree grew in the center, lending shade to the hot afternoon sun. They continued on until reaching the main entry, where several women sat.

"These are my servants. They will assist you with anything that you might need." He swung his arm wide, indicating everyone in the room.

"I'm not sure I need so much help." Charlotte stared at the women, giving them a tentative smile.

Ahmose squeezed her hand. "This is how I live in Thebes. Later we will visit my brother's harem. He will be anxious to meet you."

Charlotte pictured a houseful of naked women running around feeding the men grapes. She knew she was just being childish. This was how ancient Egyptians lived—at least the ones who had money.

"Do you have a harem?" she asked without thinking.

Ahmose turned to her. "You are standing in my harem."

Charlotte's gut clenched. "B-but I thought these women were your servants, not your wives." Her gaze traveled over their faces once again, jealously scrutinizing their appearance.

Ahmose tipped her chin back until she was looking at him. "A harem is private quarters. A retreat. These women are my servants. You will be my wife."

Charlotte leaned into the warmth she saw in his eyes. His gaze held so much promise, so much...*love*? She knew it wasn't possible, but there it was in the depths of his black eyes—love. He'd just met her. There was no way he could be feeling such things. It couldn't happen, she wouldn't allow it.

What are you going to do, rip out his heart? The thought had her cringing. If she stayed here for much longer it could very well happen when she left.

"Come, my love. Let us eat." Ahmose clapped his hands twice and the women scattered in all directions.

Within moments a linen throw had been tossed on the floor and an area had been set up for them to dine. Bowls containing dried fish, fresh fruit, and bread were laid upon the blanketed floor. Cushions stuffed with goose feathers were brought for them to sit upon. A thick beverage was poured into two cups; the servants tossed in dates and stirred in honey. One was handed to Ahmose, the other to Charlotte. He held up his cup and waited for her to do the same.

"Here's to my future bride." He grinned and took a sip.

Charlotte smiled back and drank from her cup. The brew was thick and grainy as it slid down her throat. She'd read about this drink, but this was the first time she'd ever tasted barley beer. From the darkness and the taste of the brew, it was quite a potent batch. As Charlotte drank, her muscles begin to relax. Ahmose tore off a bit of the crusty bread and handed it to her, then passed the fish.

"How long have you lived here?" Charlotte asked, sounding too eager. There was so much she wanted to learn, so much she wanted to see.

"Many years." He swallowed the bread he'd been chewing. "My brother and I were raised in the town of Gurob, near the Fayuum oasis on the edge of the desert. My family has another harem palace there. Perhaps you'd like to see it sometime?"

"I'd love to." Charlotte couldn't hide the enthusiasm in her voice.

This whole experience was like a dream come true. She was afraid at any moment she'd awaken and it would all be gone. Charlotte's heart squeezed in her chest and for a moment she had to look away, unable to gaze into Ahmose's eyes. After a few seconds, she composed herself enough to continue their conversation.

"Would it be possible to view the city of Thebes today?" *Did she really have time to sightsee? But how could she be here and not?*

Ahmose was watching her closely, not missing the moment her eyes misted over. "I think that would be possible. My chariot is housed with my horses."

Excitement filled Charlotte.

"Tell me, my love, where do your people hail from?"

Charlotte stilled mid-motion from picking up her cup to take a drink. She'd hoped they could avoid this question. She put the beer down, her teeth worrying her bottom lip. Finally she released a breath.

"I come from lands far to the north, beyond the realms of Egypt, across the seas." She began picking at a loose thread on her kilt.

"How did you come to be here?" Ahmose took a drink of his beer, and then set the cup down.

That was a very good question and for the life of her, Charlotte wished she had the answer. She couldn't exactly blurt out she was from a different time. Ahmose would probably have her stoned to death. So she fibbed. "My people left me on their journey further south."

His brows furrowed and anger flashed in his black gaze. "How could they leave the bearer of the Tears of Amun and one so fine and beautiful as you?"

Charlotte glanced down at her lap, then back up into his face. "Where I'm from the Tears of Amun don't have the same meaning."

"How can that be?" He shook his head. "The gods would not allow it."

"My people have moved away from the gods. They are not as well thought of as they are here."

Ahmose gasped. "This cannot be. It is blasphemous." He rose from the floor, his hands going to his hips. "I do not understand your people."

Charlotte chuckled. "If it makes you feel any better, I don't either."

"Come." He held out his hand. "Let me show you Thebes."

Charlotte let Ahmose pull her to her feet. He led her behind the palace to a stable. There were many horses of various colors in a paddock, and off to the side stood five chariots.

"Are those all yours?" She pointed to the chariots.

Ahmose grinned. "They are mine and my family's. The one on the end is my favorite."

Charlotte could see why it was his favorite. The front of the chariot was inlaid in gilded gold. The wood paneling at the sides had been painted and carved with depictions of Ahmose defeating his enemies in battle. The vehicle was so ornate, Charlotte wondered if they should really be riding in it.

"Come." He tugged her arm, pulling her forward. "What color do you prefer?"

Ahmose nodded toward the horses. Her gaze flew to the massive horseflesh prancing around the ring, kicking up sand. A dappled gray stallion bucked and reared, nickering loudly, drawing her attention from the others. His long white mane and tail glowed in the sunlight. The muscles in his sleek body rippled with unbridled strength. He tossed his head in her direction, then snorted.

"Him." She pointed to the stud.

Ahmose smiled again. "He's my favorite. I call him Hasani. It means handsome."

Charlotte glanced back into the paddock. "It fits him," she said, laughing.

Ahmose whistled, three quick bursts of sound. Hasani's ears twitched then perked up. Ahmose repeated the whistle and the stallion trotted over to stand next to him.

"That's a great trick." She nodded toward the horse. "Do they all do that?"

It was Ahmose's turn to laugh. "Only when they feel like it, I'm afraid. They are much like women — they do nothing unless they want to."

Charlotte opened her mouth to protest.

Ahmose winked, immediately soothing her ruffled feathers.

Heat rose in her cheeks. How did he calm her so easily? She shook her head and rolled her eyes. Ahmose leaned in and kissed her on the cheek, then signaled for his servants to ready the chariot.

Moments later, wind whipped through Charlotte's hair as they raced down the roads of Thebes. Several people lined the streets to see the chariot pass by. Hasani's slashing hooves and the chariot's wheels clattering over the stones sent dust whipping behind them. Ahmose had her pressed to the front of the chariot, his weight balanced behind her as he guided the conveyance. Charlotte could feel his cock against her back, as it grew and lengthened with every move she made.

She felt strong, powerful, like a woman. Not the klutzy girl she'd been when she left her time. She wiggled and his shaft grew, hard and urgent. He groaned, dropping one hand to his side. Suddenly she felt a tug at the back of her kilt and then a breeze. She froze.

"What are you doing?"

He pressed his lips to her ear. "Spread your legs a little more." He rasped his fingernails over her silky skin, leaving gooseflesh in its place.

Without thinking, Charlotte did, exposing her cunny to his machinations. Ahmose slipped inside her from behind, filling her completely, before taking up the reins once more. Each bump they hit drove his thick cock deeper into her core. The slow torturous movements seared her, fanning out across her body like licking flames. Charlotte tried to wiggle around so she could see him.

"Don't move." His hips pressed against her, holding her to the front of the chariot. The pressure caused her clitoris to throb. "Or someone may notice," he whispered, taking care to steer the chariot over the uneven road.

She couldn't breathe or think, only feel as she gripped the chariot, as he continued to slip in and out of her wet pussy. Her nipples stabbed against the linen, rasping. Ahmose placed the reins in one hand and circled her clitoris with the other. His thumb probed and stroked, feathering the nubbin with glorious attention. Charlotte's cunny pulsed once, then she came hard. Her scream was muffled, swallowed by his rapacious kiss. He thrust rapidly, driving into her like a man possessed, before following her shortly thereafter.

This was one chariot ride she wouldn't soon forget. Deliciously sated, it took Charlotte a few moments to realize that they had passed the temple at Karnak. Sand dried out her mouth, but she didn't want the ride to end. She breathed in, the heavy spice from nearby kitchens perfumed the air. Charlotte could almost taste the food from the odor alone.

Ahmose slowed Hasani to a trot, his hooves clopping, as they echoed off the walls of the many shops and homes tucked throughout Thebes. The sun was setting on the horizon, brilliant rays of red, purple, and pink, catching the sails from the boats on the Nile in its fading light. Charlotte sighed and snuggled deeper against Ahmose's chest, a smile planted on her face. She could get used to this way of life quite easily. The thought should scare the wits out of her, but it didn't.

They returned to the palace as the last rays of light dropped below the horizon. Ahmose helped her down from the chariot and handed the reins to one of his servants.

"Come, it is time to break for the night." He guided her along the path, his big hand resting on the small of her back.

Charlotte could feel heat from his touch through her clothes as if he'd placed a hot iron against her skin. Her stomach knotted in anticipation. Ahmose didn't look at her, but she could tell he was aware of her slightest movement. They entered the palace, passing through the main parlor area, out into the courtyard beyond, and then into the chamber that held his sleeping area.

Charlotte couldn't seem to remember how to walk. She tripped over one stone and then another, until Ahmose clasped her elbow, steadying her.

His singeing touch only served to intensify the emotions she was feeling. Her skin burned. Was it possible to spontaneously combust? At the moment, Charlotte thought so. She tugged at the material near her neck. Her clothing felt as if it were smothering her, every fiber woven together to add to her discomfort. She glanced out of the corner of her eye and caught Ahmose smiling at her. She didn't think this situation was in the least bit funny.

"Are you warm, my love?" He leaned in until his lips were almost upon her ear.

Charlotte shivered.

"I can help," he all but growled. "Perhaps you'd like some water?" His eyes twinkled in the torch-lit hallway.

She shot him a look. Ahmose didn't even flinch. He was enjoying the fact that he could toy with her. He knew she was at the mercy of her hormones. Well two could play that game. Charlotte knew she may not have much experience, but if the chariot ride was any indication, she wasn't completely without means.

Charlotte ran her hand along Ahmose's arm, pausing at his rounded shoulder. His muscles tensed beneath her fingertips, but he did not pull away. She continued her innocent exploration onto his chest, his skin searing her hand. When she reached the flat disc of his nipple Charlotte rubbed it between her thumb and forefinger. Ahmose's breath caught and his eyes flashed.

"You are playing a dangerous game, little one. Everyone knows not to tease a lion." His grin was absolutely feral.

She gave him a wide-eyed look as if to say she didn't know what he was talking about, and worked her hand lower. Charlotte's fingers slid over the ridges of Ahmose's muscled stomach. When she arrived at his navel, he flinched. This was fun. Having this big strong male at her mercy was more enjoyable than she'd thought it could be.

She circled his belly button, allowing her nails to lightly scrape his skin. Charlotte slid her hand along his belted waist. She glanced down and saw the evidence of his arousal pushing against the white linen of his kilt.

His cock grew thicker the longer she stared. Finally Charlotte couldn't resist. She slipped her hand over his shaft. Ahmose froze for a second and then pressed his length into her hand. Charlotte's fingers wrapped around his cock. His breath came hissing out.

"Are you trying to cause injury to me?" he asked, his voice hoarse.

"No." Charlotte went to pull her hand back, but he stopped her.

He took a deep breath and let it out. "I was trying to be gentle with you since today was your first time. But such torture is driving all honorable thoughts from my head." His body trembled beneath her touch. Ahmose's gaze bulleted to her lips. "Ra, give me strength." He groaned and leaned down, pressing his lips to hers. The kiss was gentle, not rushed, as if they had all the time in the world.

She didn't think there would ever be a moment when she would tire of his embraces. Her knees quivered as he deepened the kiss, his mouth firming as hers grew more yielding. His tongue swiped at her lower lip, seeking entrance. Charlotte opened for him, welcoming his spicy taste. His hands moved to her shoulders. He rested his palms there for but a moment then pulled her closer without shifting her hand from his shaft.

Charlotte felt his cock pulse against her fingers. Tentatively she stroked down, unsure of exactly what to do. He bucked his hips in encouragement. She reversed direction and slid her hand back up his length. Ahmose growled against her mouth. Feeling confident, Charlotte stroked him again, this time without pausing. His grip on her shoulders increased, but he didn't break the kiss. She increased her speed, enjoying the feel of his fullness in her hand.

Sweat broke out on Ahmose's brow. He was trying very hard not to drag her to the ground right in the hallway. His fingers bit into the material around her shoulders, trying to anchor his need. She slid her silken fingers over his crown and gently applied pressure. He clenched his jaw against his instinctive response to thrust. If she kept this up for much longer he was going to spill his essence. Unable to take a minute more, Ahmose pulled back from the kiss, gasping.

"Woman, you have tortured me long enough."

He grabbed her hand, pulling Charlotte more forcefully than he'd intended toward his bedchamber. He was loosening the ties holding her kilt together before they even reached the door. Her lips were swollen and red from his kisses. Ahmose snatched up a wisp of her curly hair and brought it to his nose. She smelled of wind and sunshine. Her eyes were wide and sparkling in the torchlight.

He released her long enough to shut the door. He then walked to a small bowl containing myrrh and frankincense, crushing the resin in his hand until the room smelled of spice. He turned in time to see Charlotte remove the remaining linen from her body. Ahmose's breath caught. Her skin glowed like alabaster. The rose of her engorged nipples called out to him. The dark thatch of curls between her thighs had already begun to dampen, glistening like a beacon in the torchlight.

She wanted him, just as much as he wanted her.

His mouth watered at the thought of sinking between her spread legs and sampling of her bounty once again. Tasting her juices as they burst from her body in ecstasy. His cock strained beneath the material of his kilt, demanding to be released. The Tears of Amun adorned her neck, while the ruby earrings flashed fire against her ears. Ahmose swallowed hard. He longed for the moment to last for this lifetime and into the next. He fisted his hands at his sides to keep from reaching out and taking her. He wasn't done looking his fill.

Charlotte shifted under his intense gaze. Inside her a fire raged that only he could douse. She had no idea what possessed her, but she brought her finger to her mouth, gave it a quick lick, then ran the same finger around her nipple, leaving a trail of moisture. The areola puckered. Ahmose's nostrils flared and his body trembled. He removed his kilt in a few seconds flat and was upon her. This time his kiss was aggressive, hungry. He pushed past her defenses, attacking her mouth savagely.

Charlotte was lost. His hands seemed to be everywhere at once, groping, pinching, squeezing, and caressing. He kneaded her flesh, stroking her mons at the same time. Charlotte moaned against his mouth. He dipped one finger into her drenched channel and began to thrust in and out. When her hips joined in the rhythm he added another finger. The tension in her abdomen was building, drawing nearer to release. She tightened her inner muscles, holding his hand in place, seeking the relief he promised.

Just when she was about to slip over the edge he broke the kiss and pulled out of her, maneuvering her toward the bed. Charlotte went to lie down, but Ahmose stopped her. Instead he spun her and bent her forward until only her elbows rested on the reed mats. Charlotte's heart leapt to her throat and her breath seized. Visions of the chariot ride passed through her mind, fueling her need.

For a few seconds she stood there, her bottom raised in the air toward Ahmose. Then she felt his cock as it brushed against her cheeks, hard like granite, yet soft as satin. He didn't try to enter her. He just continued to stroke over her skin, teasing the edge of her pussy lips. Charlotte pushed back in encouragement. He laughed and held her hips still. He leaned down and placed a kiss on each globe. Charlotte trembled.

Ahmose stood, and then bent over her. "You have punished me long enough," he whispered against her hair. "Now it is my turn."

Excitement thrummed through her. She could feel her nipples bead to the point of pain. Her cunny was saturated to the point that her dew was about to run down her legs. And not for one second did Charlotte care, her sole focus on the large cock between Ahmose's thighs, and the sexy voice vibrating through her senses. Her clitoris twitched as he slid the crown over her nub, his heavy sac brushing her leg. Charlotte bit her lip to keep from crying out, or worse yet, begging.

Ahmose stuck the tip of his cock in her waiting entrance, his fingers digging into the flesh of her hips in preparation. He would torture her for a few minutes more and then fuck her senseless. He pulled out and she whimpered, opening her legs wider.

"Is there something you wanted to say to me, my love?"

Charlotte groaned. "No."

He dipped inside once more, this time releasing one hip so that he could reach around and massage her clitoris. Charlotte whimpered, her legs almost giving out. Ahmose circled her stomach, holding her up with one hand. He rocked forward again, his shaft sliding past her entrance and along her crack. She bucked within his hold, her cunny demanding his cock.

"Please," she begged.

"That's all I wanted to hear." His voice was gravelly as he released her long enough to grab her hips once more and plunge in from behind, branding her.

Charlotte screamed as an orgasm racked her body, pulsing and throbbing as wave after wave hit her. She could hear the suction noise as Ahmose drove his cock in and out of her pussy, his heavy sac slapping against her skin. His hips thrust against her bottom, lifting her up onto her toes. Charlotte bore down to take him deep inside. It was his turn to groan. She clamped her muscles tight around his cock, slowing his movements.

"Charlotte, if you do that again, I will spill." His voice was strained.

She smiled, considering it for a moment, then squeezed. Ahmose gripped her tighter and then thrust one more time, a cry dying on his lips. His hips continued to flex and move. She could feel his hot seed spurting into her body, filling her womb. For a moment the thought panicked her, but then Charlotte realized if she got pregnant, it would be okay because she'd be carrying Ahmose's child.

"You are truly a sorceress, my love." He dragged in a ragged breath. "And I thank the gods that you are mine."

Charlotte rested her head on the bed. She wasn't sure if when she moved, her legs would support her. Sweat dripped down her back and under her breasts. Her pussy lips felt pouty and swollen. The room smelled of spice and sex…their sex. Their lovemaking was the sweetest aroma she'd ever inhaled.

Ahmose lifted her from behind and placed her on the bed. He gathered the rumpled covers before slipping in beside her and pulling Charlotte tight against his smooth chest.

Chapter Four

∞

The next day Ahmose had the chariot waiting. They were off to the city of Gurob to the harem palace.

The ride through the countryside was breathtaking—fertile fields, the Nile in the distance. Charlotte closed her eyes for a moment trying to store the picture in her mind for eternity. The air was clean and lightly scented with flowers.

Ahmose led her past several temples on the journey to middle Egypt, each one more spectacular than the last. He pointed out the fact that most were still under construction and would continue to be for years to come, because honoring the gods took time. Charlotte wished she could tell him that these temples would be much loved for thousands of years.

They arrived at the harem palace a couple hours later. Ahmose had stopped along the way to greet the people, taking time to enter fields and help out where needed. From what Charlotte could see he was well liked and well respected by all, winning over everyone who crossed his path. *No wonder you were able to unite the kingdoms of Egypt.* Her admiration and love for him grew stronger by the minute.

* * * * *

The palace was smaller than the one he lived in at Thebes, but far homier. Trees from the nearby oasis flourished, their thick, dense leaves shading much of the dwelling. Plump dates were cultivated in the fields, giving the air a sweet, fruity aroma. Grass the color of emeralds grew abundant enough to allow Hasani to graze.

A beautiful woman greeted them at the door, her skin the color of roasted almonds, and a regal countenance that was born, not learned. Her eyes were the same black fire as Ahmose's. She wore a perfectly braided ebony wig and immaculate white linens draped over her pert nipples and lithe form. Jealousy streaked through Charlotte and her stomach knotted as she pictured Ahmose sinking his cock into this beautiful woman's cunt. His head buried between the woman's spread thighs lapping at her plump folds until she screamed out an earth shattering release. Charlotte fisted her hands.

"King Kamose is not here. He is visiting his fields."

Ahmose nodded, kissed the woman on the cheek, then immediately pulled Charlotte forward. "I'd like you to meet my mother, Ashotep."

The woman smiled and rushed forward to embrace her, pushing Ahmose to the side. Charlotte's discomfort faded instantly, replaced by embarrassment. And to think she'd actually considered throttling the woman. Ashotep tugged Charlotte's hands, hurrying her inside, and out of the hot midday sun.

"Ahmose sent word that his chosen one had arrived, but I did not believe it until I saw you with my own eyes," his mother said, her smile growing.

She wasn't quite sure how to respond to what Ashotep had just told her. When had Ahmose found time to send a message?

"It is not everyday that a son brings home his future bride," Ashotep continued, her voice rising with excitement.

She glanced over her shoulder at Ahmose, her eyes narrowing. He raised his eyebrows in innocence. "It's very nice to meet you." She squeezed the woman's hands before releasing them.

Charlotte tried to imagine her mother in the same position. Would Victoria enthusiastically welcome Ahmose as her soon to be son-in-law? She doubted it. Not unless he came with a pile of ancient gold relics and the keys to Egypt.

Ashotep's smile deepened. "We will break bread and then you can tell us about you. There is much to prepare in such a short time."

Charlotte's brows furrowed.

"You must be excited about your wedding," Ashotep gushed.

Charlotte's stomach twisted, forming a bundle of nerves. Could she really go through with this? As much as she'd like to spend her life with Ahmose, she would feel guilty leaving her parents without a word. *If she could even return to her own time…*

The conversation was lively as they dined. Ahmose's mother told tales of the trouble he used to get into when he was a little boy. Charlotte glanced at him from beneath her lashes. It wasn't hard to imagine Ahmose as a little boy with those big black eyes and ebony hair. He probably charmed his way out of getting punished. His children would be exact copies of him. Her heart squeezed in her chest at the thought of Ahmose with kids.

He would be a good father, patient and loving, yet firm. She swallowed the bread she'd been chewing, and it lodged in her throat. It wouldn't do to think about such things. Once she was gone, he'd move on, find himself an Egyptian bride and go on to rule Egypt. Logically Charlotte knew that was the way things should happen, but no matter how many times she tried to convince herself, she still couldn't picture Ahmose with anyone but her. The thought of another woman wrapping her body around him nauseated her.

A few hours later, they said their goodbyes. Ashotep promised to help with the wedding plans and assured Charlotte she was marrying a prince of a man. No one had to convince Charlotte. Ahmose was everything she could ever want in a husband. He'd had her at the first glance.

They rode back to the palace in Thebes as the sun lowered on the horizon. The sounds of families in their homes wafted into the streets, their voices rising high with laughter. Spice filled the air as the various kitchens were put to good use.

"What are you thinking?" Ahmose whispered near her ear.

"I'm thinking how wonderful a place Egypt is and how great the people are." She smiled to herself.

A land she'd helped uncover from the sands of time now rose proudly before her like a sentinel standing guard at the gates of heaven. If she did end up returning to her own time, no one would believe the tale she'd tell, certainly not her parents. Charlotte knew without a doubt she'd never be able to breathe a word without fear of being locked away.

* * * * *

That evening Ahmose was especially romantic in his lovemaking. He anointed her body with myrrh-scented oil, pouring it from a Syrian inspired vessel. His hands were gentle as he smoothed the liquid over her shoulders and down her arms, carefully avoiding her beaded nipples and aching clitoris. He rubbed oil into her legs and over her buttocks, kneading them firmly as he made his way up her back. Ahmose rubbed until the last of the kinks were gone.

She was practically swaying with need when his palms finally made contact with her nipples. He brushed the pads of his thumbs over the rose-tipped peaks and they grew rigid with desire. Her breathing came out in ragged gasps. He continued to play with her full mounds, molding and shaping.

Charlotte's channel flooded and she mewed. She shifted to stave off the ache. It only added to the friction. When Ahmose leaned down and whisked his tongue across her stiff crests, she almost came.

He suckled her tortured peak, tugging with his lips, then his teeth. When she thought she could stand no more Ahmose switched to her other nipple. He fed hungrily, flicking his tongue, capturing it again and again as if this were the last time they'd get to lie together. She moaned. He pushed her back toward the bed without breaking contact. Her nipples were engorged by the time he'd settled her on the edge of the reed mat.

Charlotte's breathing was choppy at best. Her breasts throbbed and tingled as heat raced over her oiled skin, centering at the juncture between her spread thighs. Ahmose dropped to his knees before her, then slipped his hands behind her and pulled her forward until her pussy was level with his mouth. He glanced up from beneath long lashes and smiled. The act was simply carnal, telling Charlotte without words that he was about to eat her alive. Her clitoris pulsed.

Ahmose leaned forward and inhaled. "Your scent drives me wild. I feel like an animal when you are near."

Dew dripped down the soft curls between Charlotte's spread legs, inviting him to drink deep. She smelled musky and aroused, the oil of myrrh only adding to her allure. She bit her lip as he dipped his head closer and gently blew warm air on her heated flesh. Charlotte shivered, her nipples jutting out like ripe fruit fresh for the picking. Ahmose lifted one leg and slipped it over his shoulder, then repeated the action with her other, tipping her cunny toward his face.

"Do you know how much I long to taste you and touch you?" he growled in the back of his throat. "You are so beautiful, I'm surprised Ra has not come to claim you for himself."

He smiled again, letting Charlotte see the fire that she'd ignited inside him, the passion that burned unending; the need that screamed out from his cock, and the love that he felt in his heart. She was his and he was hers. That was how it was and how it should be.

Ahmose leaned forward and swiped his tongue over her swollen lips. Charlotte shuddered and closed her eyes. He could feel her body's tension, the underlying desperation, and the overall yearning hidden deep inside.

"Food shall never taste the same to me from this day forth. For it could never compare to the bounty between your thighs."

He laved her again, circling her hot wet sheath, teasing her pussy with his tongue. Her tender flesh responded by dampening more and puffing out. Ahmose, intoxicated by her scent, swayed drunkenly with her responsiveness. He dove in, uncovering the hidden jewel lying beneath her heated folds.

Charlotte's nails bit into his shoulders as he sucked the bud into his mouth and gently worried it with his teeth. She gasped, unable to catch her breath.

"Ahmose…" She groaned.

He circled her clitoris with his tongue, sliding it back and forth in imitation of a snake. It was all it took to send her over the edge.

"I'm coming…"

Her channel flooded, wetting his chin, and still Ahmose fed, lapping up every last drop of her release.

Charlotte threw her head back and screamed. Her body convulsed as her orgasm slammed down upon her. Ahmose's face lay buried between her legs, devouring her. She couldn't seem to control the shudders racking her body. Her vision faded to black and she blinked to gain back her senses. Her skin was alive and pulsing as contraction after contraction rocked her.

She lay back on the bed waiting for her breathing to return to normal. Ahmose stayed between her legs, placing tender kisses upon her thighs. It took several minutes before Charlotte could piece together a coherent sentence. When she did, she sat up on her elbows and kept it short.

"My turn," she purred, licking her lips and pulling him up onto the bed beside her.

Ahmose lay on his back, his arms covering his eyes. His cock was hard enough to pound gold. He didn't think he'd ever tire of feeding from Charlotte's endless well. She was ambrosia, sweeter than the finest wines in Egypt and more precious than all his gold and gems combined. Her taste simmered in his mouth, tempting his appetite. Her breathing had finally slowed to a satisfied purr. Ahmose contented himself with the fact that he'd been able to please her as no other.

He grinned and was just about to turn to tell her when he felt her lips slip over the crown of his cock. The air seemed to freeze in his lungs. Unable to gasp or speak, he waited. Her touch was tentative at first, a quick lick followed by a gentle suck. Ahmose held as still as the dead, forcing himself to keep from thrusting. When he was finally able to draw air it was on a gasp.

"Does that feel all right?" Her voice quavered as she spoke around his cock.

Ahmose uncovered his eyes and looked down at her. "It feels like a thousand tiny butterflies have alighted on my staff."

Charlotte licked him from balls to tip and back again. "Do you like it when I suck you?"

Ahmose groaned. "You have no idea."

She took him into her mouth and began to suck. Ahmose's muscles tightened and he gripped the sheets. She swirled her tongue over the sensitive head, sliding it around his length. The pressure of her mouth increased, coinciding with the building pressure inside Ahmose. He felt his sac rise, drawing near his body, ready for release. Charlotte's fingers slipped around the base of his cock and she began matching rhythm with her mouth. The combination of her wetness with the silky smoothness of her skin was too much for him.

"You must stop," he gritted out between clenched teeth.

She shook her head without breaking stride, increasing the speed of her motions.

"I can't hold back." He gasped, the muscles in his abdomen contracting.

"Mmm," she purred over his cock.

Ahmose almost came off the bed. He grasped her silky hair, at the same time thrusting up into her molten mouth. The searing heat combined with the pressure from her sucking sent shockwaves through his body. His cock rejoiced. He jerked and thrust once more, then sent his seed jettisoning out into her mouth and down her throat. Charlotte didn't try to pull back. Instead she drank deep. Ahmose trembled and quaked, his body exhausted.

He pulled Charlotte up beside him. "You are amazing."

She blushed. "Do you really think so?"

He brushed a wisp of hair off her face and kissed her. "I know so."

* * * * *

The days passed quickly, leading up to the Opet festival, where the pharaoh would be reborn. The celebration would also signal the return of Sopdet, a bright star on the horizon, marking the Egyptian New Year.

Charlotte's wedding day had arrived. So blissfully in love, she'd decided even if the opportunity to return to her own time should appear, she would not take it. Her life, her heart, and her future happiness were here with Ahmose.

Her soon to be husband had given her token gifts of his affection every day since she'd arrived. His lavish presents, like his love, were endless. Ahmose asked for nothing in exchange. Yet Charlotte couldn't assuage the guilt she felt about not being able to gift him back. She knew that the act of giving presents was a large part of the marriage ceremony. She ran her hand over the Tears of Amun and a chill skittered over her. She quickly dismissed the feeling as wedding jitters.

The city of Thebes was abuzz about the festival. Preparations had begun early in the week and were now culminating. Tonight, the people of Egypt would gather at the temple of Karnak, bringing out Amun, his wife Mut, and their son Khonsu's statues on sacred barques. They'd then be carried in procession along the sphinx-lined route that connected Karnak to Luxor. Worshipers believed that at the Luxor temple, in the inner sanctuary, Amun would ritually unite with

Ahmose's mother so that she could again give birth to the royal *Ka*.

When the ceremony ended King Kamose would enter the sanctuary, merging with his newborn *Ka*. He would later reappear, replenished with divine power, as the son of Amun-Ra. King Kamose would then receive the crowds. Dancers would perform and great offerings of meat and bread would be made. Once presented and ultimately enjoyed by the gods, the bounty would be distributed to the people.

Charlotte was excited about the celebration, but dread had settled into her bones like an anchor, pulling her down despite her enthusiasm. Ashotep had brought a special gown from Gurob with her and had fashioned an elegant wig for Charlotte's head. She assured Charlotte that she looked beautiful, and then escorted her to the courtyard of the palace where Ahmose was waiting.

Charlotte's breath caught when she spotted Ahmose. So handsome, so regal. He stood loose-limbed near a fig tree with a small crown of gold on his wigged head. Ahmose wore a fresh, embroidered kilt that had been fashioned and inlayed with precious gems. A scarab of gold graced his ring finger. His hands were at his sides. Despite his relaxed appearance, his shoulders looked tense. His eyes sought hers, holding, confirming she was truly there, and only then did he appear to relax.

The ceremony, which amounted to little more than holding hands and declaring one's intentions, was over within minutes. By the time they'd finished, Charlotte's head was swimming. She didn't know if it was fear or exhilaration. Either way, it was over and nothing would come between them. Charlotte turned to her husband and placed a chaste kiss upon his lips.

"Remember always, I love you."

Ahmose's fingers trembled as he brought them to her face. "You have nothing to fear now. It is done."

Charlotte breathed a sigh of relief, trying to ignore the lingering dread, lurking like a shadow in the back of her mind. It seemed to be growing in intensity, like a storm on the horizon, moving swiftly, decimating everything in its path. Charlotte pushed it aside and smiled at Ahmose. *It's just wedding jitters.* They would eventually die down and she'd forget about them, so they could enjoy the Opet festival tonight.

Ashotep left to prepare herself for her part in the rituals. Ahmose pulled Charlotte into his arms and kissed her deeply. "You are now mine—all mine and no one can take you away," he whispered against her lips, rocking her from side to side. Eventually his head came to rest on top of hers.

Charlotte could feel the tension in his muscles. "You feel it too, don't you?"

His muscles locked, holding her tight. "I feel nothing, but happiness on this day."

Despite his words of assurance, Charlotte sensed that he seemed reluctant to release her.

Chapter Five

၅ာ

The festival was a joyous occasion. Charlotte joined Ahmose and his family in the royal entourage as they made their way from Karnak to Luxor temple. The mood was jubilant, yet sedated. It should have been the happiest day of her life, but she couldn't seem to bring herself to celebrate. Ahmose strolled silently beside her, his hand holding her own. Strength poured off him in waves as he silently sent her reassurances.

Charlotte stayed close, afraid to release him for fear her dream would fade away. Which was ridiculous—she'd already been here for nearly a week. She'd found no way back in that time, nor desired to return.

The crowd gathered outside the temple, their hushed voices chanting in unison. Ahmose's mother had been inside the sanctuary for several hours by now, convening with the gods. His brother, King Kamose, stepped forward and entered the temple.

The full moon glowed yellow in the sky, its shimmering light abundant, making the use of torches all but unnecessary. An hour later King Kamose emerged, vibrant. The crowd broke out of their reverie, cheering and rushing forward quickly to make their offerings.

With the gods appeased, the mood turned outright hedonistic. Wine flowed freely, along with barley beer. Platters of bread, fish, gazelle, and geese were passed around to everyone to sample. Ahmose gathered food for them, then pulled Charlotte away from the crowd.

He stuck his mouth next to her left ear. "I'm selfish. I want you to myself."

They strolled back toward the temple of Karnak, passing revelers along the way. The moonlight glistened upon the waters of the Nile. In the distance, clouds gathered on the horizon, heralding an incoming storm. The breeze picked up, carrying perfumed oils and cypress grass in its wake. Hand-in-hand they walked back. Ahmose took Charlotte around the temple until they were standing next to the sacred lake.

"I wanted to return to the place where I first laid eyes on you, so that I can offer the gods my thanks." He spoke low and deep as he pulled her back against his chest, his arms wrapping around her waist.

Charlotte shivered as a raindrop spattered her face. "This place will always hold fond memories for me, also." She squeezed his hands. "It's where I met the man I've loved for as long as I can remember."

She didn't have to see his frown to feel it. The tension in his body increased tenfold. "How could you have loved me for years, when I just met you a few sunrises ago?"

Charlotte turned in his arms until she faced him. The moon was so bright she could easily make out his features, even with clouds closing in. "What is important is that we've found each other and we're in love." She framed his face with her hands and rose up on tiptoe to kiss him once more.

"You are my love," he said when she pulled back. "My only love."

Charlotte bit her lip and then smiled. "There's something I want to give you."

Ahmose stilled her hands as she moved toward her neck. "That is not necessary, Charlotte. You are gift enough." He lifted her chin and began to nibble on her lips.

"I can't think when you do that, you know."

He laughed. "That is the purpose."

"Ahmose..." He continued to feast upon her mouth. "Ahmose, please."

He stilled. Lightning flashed in the distance, followed by a loud crack of thunder. Charlotte looked warily at the incoming storm before turning back to Ahmose.

"You've given me so much. I want to show you how much you mean to me."

He frowned for a moment and then sighed. "If that is what you wish, I will accept your gift."

Charlotte reached for the clasp on the Tears of Amun. It seemed to catch for a moment before slipping free. Ahmose turned and allowed her to put it on him. The air around them turned electric.

Facing her once again, he asked, "What do you think? I'm sure it looks better upon you."

Charlotte smiled, as a wave of dizziness washed over her. "I lov—aahhh!" The scream ripped from her insides.

Pain shot through her and she couldn't seem to focus, as if a spike were being driven through her skull. Rain started to fall in sheets. Charlotte could see Ahmose's lips moving, his eyes rounded in fear. He struggled to grasp hold of her, but couldn't seem to do so. Her gold wedding ring dropped from her hand. The storm raged around them. His handsome face swam before her eyes. One minute he was there.

The next he was gone.

"Noooo…" Charlotte cried out, but it was too late. Lightning flashed nearby, rattling her teeth. She was falling. Falling back toward the water. Back into the sacred lake. "Ahmose, I love you," she shouted one more time, praying that her words reached him.

* * * * *

Charlotte broke the water's surface, sputtering, her mouth full of moss. The sun was shining brightly and it took a few seconds before she was actually able to see. Her hair was plastered to her head, sans the wig she'd been wearing. She knew without looking that Ahmose was not with her. She wiped her face and pulled herself from the water. Her heart and body ached as if she were being torn asunder.

"Where have you been, young lady?" a shrill voice behind her asked.

Charlotte closed her eyes and took a deep breath before turning to face her mother. The sun was shining brightly, heating the air to oven temperatures. Her heart ached to the point of bursting.

"What did you do to your dress?" The frown on her mother's face would have wilted flowers and seemed to be deepening by the second. "What on earth are you wearing? It's positively scandalous."

Charlotte glanced down and vaguely registered the fact she was still wearing her Egyptian kilt. Her body was unadorned of jewelry; it seemed the precious metal could not survive time-travel. *Except the Tears of Amun.*

"I'm glad we decided to come looking for you when you didn't show up to help. Goodness knows what we would have found had we not."

Charlotte's brows knitted. "What do you mean?"

"Don't play dimwitted with me, Charlotte Constance Witherspoon." Her mother stepped forward then stopped, her eyes narrowing on the front of Charlotte's wrap.

Charlotte glanced down and gasped. Her shirt had once again gone sheer, except this time she wore nothing underneath to disguise her nakedness. The sound of heavy feet caught her attention. Field workers rushed forward, their harried voices growing louder as they approached.

"Goodness…" Her mother sucked in a surprised breath as she glanced over her shoulder. "Henry, get down here this instant! And for heaven's sake lend us your outer shirt. *Your* daughter is dressed like a…like a…harlot!" Victoria snapped her fingers and Henry jumped, ambling forward.

189

"I daresay, what have you gotten up to, gel?" he asked, handing over his shirt to Charlotte, his jowled features reddening beneath his hat.

Victoria harrumphed. "I know what it looks like she's been doing." She arched a fine brow, not bothering to lower her voice. Victoria pulled a handkerchief from her sleeve, bringing it to her mouth to cover her disdain.

Charlotte gazed at the crowd of workers whispering to each other, their eyes as round as saucers. Slowly she reached for the shirt her father had offered, wrapping it around her. Shivers wracked her body. "I'm sorry, Papa." She glanced down, unable to meet his eyes.

Henry's eyes softened for a moment, then he coughed. "Don't want to hear it. Don't want to hear it." His hand was waving away any chance Charlotte would be given to explain. "Can't tell you how disappointed I am."

Explain…how in the world could she do that, when she didn't even understand what had happened?

Her full week of love and happiness had passed in mere hours here. Charlotte grabbed her aching head. Her world had tilted upside down and she'd landed on the wrong side. The Tears of Amun were gone, lost in time. Since she'd placed them about Ahmose's neck there was no chance of getting them back. The pain from that realization struck deep. Charlotte began to sob.

She was well and truly stuck here.

* * * * *

Her days passed in a blur. Life with her parents had resumed a normal pace, with one exception. Charlotte was no longer allowed to travel alone without their escort. The pain Charlotte had felt upon realizing there would be no returning to her true love had turned into a dull, continuous ache. Her eyes were a permanent shade of red and the puffiness refused to go down. Of course, it didn't help that she couldn't seem to stop crying. Charlotte was convinced she'd shed enough tears to flood the Nile Valley.

She thought about Ahmose. Twelve long days had passed since she'd last laid eyes on him. In his world she'd been gone nearly three months. Had he given up on finding her? Had he already forgotten about her? Was he waiting for her to return? Had he found someone new? The last thought had her heart tripping in her chest.

Back in her own world Charlotte couldn't seem to find her feet. She'd gone through the motions at the dinner parties she'd attended with her parents. She played the doting daughter part to the teeth. All the while her stomach churned with unease. Charlotte hadn't seemed to be able to keep any food down since returning.

Tonight she was being dragged to another boring affair. Lady Alexandra Stuart had invited them to dinner, which in Victoria's eye was a big coup. Charlotte's mother had been especially diligent in watching her prepare for the evening, even going as far as to pick out a dress for her to wear. But Charlotte couldn't summon the energy to care.

* * * * *

Dinner turned out to be positively dreadful. Victoria had hoped to set her up with Lady Alexandria Stuart's son. Charlotte cringed as she recalled Robert's clammy fingers upon her hand. Raw liver was more appealing. Ahmose's touch had been so warm, firm, and gentle by comparison. Charlotte dismissed Robert unceremoniously.

By the time the evening closed and they'd reached their Model T, Victoria was fuming. "Why don't you want to see him?"

Because his touch doesn't set me aflame, make my nipples ache, my pussy throb.

"He's unsuitable, Mother. And he feels the same about me, I assure you."

Victoria gaze leveled. "You must have misunderstood him. Robert is from good stock, quite good blood. He wouldn't think such a thing."

"Believe what you want, Mother." Charlotte didn't bother to hide the exasperation in her voice.

Victoria's features hardened. "It's no wonder he thinks such things with the fodder going about town. Your virtue is in question."

Charlotte laughed; she couldn't help it. Her virtue was long gone. She pictured Ahmose above her, driving his thick cock inside her willing body. Charlotte knew she'd done nothing wrong, but still the guilt over dragging her family name through the muck pervaded. She considered apologizing, when her stomach suddenly rolled and lurched.

"Pull over please," she begged in desperation.

"We shall not," her mother vetoed.

Charlotte gripped the door. "I'm going to be ill." She threw the door open and leaned her head out in time to lose the entire contents of her stomach.

Afterwards, Charlotte slumped back down on the seat, staring out into the night.

"Gracious, Charlotte, what is the matter with you?" Victoria grabbed her kerchief and held it to her nose in disgust. "I believe I'll send a call out to Dr. Williams tomorrow."

"No!" Charlotte sprang to life. She had a pretty good idea what was wrong with her and she didn't need Dr. Williams confirming it. Things were bad enough between her and her parents. They didn't need to know she was carrying a two-thousand-year-old pharaoh's baby. She pulled herself together enough to look her mother in the eye. "I mean that won't be necessary mother. I'm feeling much better at the present. I believe I've just caught a bug."

Victoria eyed her suspiciously.

"Oh for Pete's sake, Victoria, leave her be," Henry grumbled.

Charlotte smiled tentatively at her father. He winked at her and then looked forward as if nothing had occurred.

Chapter Six

❧

The next day Charlotte rose early, forcing herself to keep down some toast. Her menses had not arrived, confirming her worst fear and her greatest hope…she was pregnant. Somehow, despite the circumstances and against all odds, Ahmose and she were going to have a baby. Charlotte was overjoyed that a piece of him still existed within her, yet terrified of her parent's reaction.

Charlotte frowned, unable to come up with a solution to the latter problem.

Her attention turned back to Ahmose and the life she had growing inside her. She placed her hand on her stomach. The thought of Ahmose not getting to see his child brought fresh tears to her eyes. It wasn't fair. Their love was not supposed to end this way. She pictured his face. The sadness she'd been feeling returned with a vengeance. Charlotte swallowed hard.

"I've got to be strong for you," she spoke, rubbing her belly.

An hour or so later her parents filed into the room. Her mother and father were setting off for the Cairo museum as soon as they broke their fast.

"Get your things together Charlotte, you're coming with us," Victoria stated between bites of toast and sips of tea.

"Mother…" Charlotte hesitated. "I thought perhaps I could stay home today and catch up on my studies."

Victoria stopped mid-bite and stared at her. She glanced at Charlotte's plate then back at her face. "You've eaten, so you obviously feel better. It would do you well, under the circumstances, to get some air." Victoria paused, her eyes narrowing. "Unless you aren't feeling better, in which case, I'll call for Dr. Williams."

Charlotte glanced at her plate then back up into her mother's face. There was no use arguing. "I'm feeling better," she lied.

"Well then, it's settled. Get yourself ready, we'll be leaving within an hour." Victoria dabbed her napkin at the corners of her mouth. "Besides, you'll learn a great deal more at the museum than you will in one of those books. Right, Henry?"

Her father coughed, his bushy brows rising as if trying to figure out what had been said. He looked at Charlotte and then at his wife. Charlotte followed his gaze. Her mother's frown said it all.

"Right," he blustered.

Charlotte rose from the table and went to her room to change. They were out of the house within an hour and on their way. The ride into Cairo was dusty as usual. She and her mother had to hang onto their hats as the wind picked up speed. The invisible breeze carried the odor of spice-filled cooking on its wings, triggering Charlotte's memory. She blushed as she recalled the last time she'd encountered that particular aroma. Ahmose had been standing behind her in the chariot, his hard cock filling her greedy pussy as they road through the streets of Thebes. The bumps had driven him deep inside her body until he'd actually nudged her womb. Had that been when she'd gotten pregnant?

Charlotte crossed her legs, trying to assuage the familiar ache that had begun. She missed his muscled body rising above her, his hairless chest scraping her engorged nipples, and his hips as they pistoned, sending his cock in and out of her moist sheath. Tears filled her eyes at the thought of never getting to experience those sensations again with Ahmose. They'd been so new and wonderful; she couldn't imagine life without them. At the same time, sharing her body with anyone else was out of the question. The thought was repulsive. His touch and his touch alone was what she sought.

The sky was clear and blue with the exception of a dark cloud lingering on the horizon. Since it was the flooding season that wasn't particularly unusual. By the time they arrived at the museum they were all covered in dust. Charlotte patted down her skirt and shook out her hat. She glanced at the horizon once more. The dark cloud had shifted, drawing nearer, instead of farther away. Charlotte placed her hat back on her head, instantly shading her eyes. The spot in the distance shouldn't have gotten any closer given its position when they left. She fought back a shiver, then turned her eyes away.

It's just a storm. Shivers racked her body as memories from a similar storm filled her mind. *Stop being silly.* Charlotte wiped away the gooseflesh rising on her arms and followed her parents into the museum. Past the entrance, the museum opened into a wider space. Tutankhamen had already been situated in his own private area with more objects added daily as they uncovered them.

"Come, Charlotte," her mother called out, turning toward Tut's gold.

Charlotte walked a few steps behind, her eyes fixing on several familiar items. Ahmose had owned jars like the ones she was viewing, their vibrant colors and designs still breathtaking after all those years in the ground. Charlotte longed to run her hands over the pottery and combs, anything to make herself feel closer to Ahmose and the world she'd lost.

A tug at her hand snapped her attention back.

"Really, Charlotte, must I hold your hand to get you to follow?" Her mother gazed at her, shaking her head. "I'm about ready to give up. Perhaps you should go stay with Aunt Edna in Surrey, if you're so unhappy here."

"No! I mean, no, I love Egypt. It's my home." Charlotte squeezed her mother's hand, willing her to understand.

For a moment Victoria's features softened, then just as quickly the hard mask returned. "Well then, come on." She pulled, dragging Charlotte behind.

They finished examining Howard Carter's find and then headed into the other rooms. They were less organized, a mismatch of Egyptian artifacts, some labeled, others not. The museum was still in its growing stage, and as such was still finding its feet in the world. Several of the displays were set up to depict tombs. Charlotte walked by each one, reading the markers beneath. Guards stood at the entrances of each room, their brown, mustached faces grim, ensuring no one stole any of the items. Punishment in Egypt was harsh. Just last week a man's hand was cut off for stealing coins from a wealthy sheik. The practice was positively barbaric, but served as a good deterrent to crime.

Her mother had considered protesting the Egyptian government, only to be stopped by her father. Charlotte grinned as she remembered that moment. It was the only time she could recall where her mother actually conceded to her father. A victory she knew her father would cherish for life.

Wandering without looking where she was going, Charlotte found herself in a smaller room. The air inside this area was still and musty, as if no one really came in here all that much. She glanced up. Her parents were nowhere in sight. Her mother would not be happy once she noticed Charlotte's absence. A boom sounded above the displays. The guards in the doorways glanced at each other and shifted uneasily.

Charlotte gazed around trying to place the sound. Another loud crack shattered the quiet. Hair on her arms stood on end. She stared out toward a blocked area that had earlier reflected sunlight. It now lay in shadows. Obviously the storm she'd seen on the horizon had caught up with them.

Charlotte ignored the tension in her shoulders and continued on. She glanced at several rows of papyrus, reading the stories they told. Her mind drifted back to ancient times. The peoples smiling faces, the simple joy their lives held. She closed her eyes, banishing the glorious thoughts from her head.

Whack!

Charlotte jumped as lightning struck nearby, shaking the columns in the building. One of the guards had caught her movement and now was following her with his eyes. She turned away, trying to ignore him. Her mother's voice rang out as her parents entered the room next to the one she was standing in.

"Have you seen a young lady with brown, curly hair, about so tall?"

Charlotte spun in time to see her mother interrogating the guard who'd been watching her. He slowly raised his hand and extended his finger in her direction. Charlotte harrumphed. So much for a few moments of peace. Her mother was marching toward her with Henry in tow. When she reached Charlotte, she halted.

"I thought I told you to stay with us."

"You did, Mother. I didn't realize you weren't here until just minutes ago." Charlotte kept her voice level. The sound carried easily inside the museum, much like when you were in a tomb.

"So your father and I are so insignificant that you don't notice whether we are here or not." Victoria placed her hands on her hips. Her raised voice had further caught the attention of the guards. The one who'd been watching Charlotte earlier was now moving closer.

"Of course not, Mother," Charlotte whispered, glancing over her mother's shoulder at the curious guard.

Victoria followed her gaze. Charlotte saw the guard's steps falter.

"Now where were we?" her mother asked, knowing perfectly well where they'd left off. "My mind is made up, Charlotte. I've spoken with your father and he thinks it's a good idea also. Right Henry?"

"Right, right," her father added before looking away, unable to meet Charlotte's questioning gaze.

"What's a good idea?" A lump had formed in Charlotte's throat as she forced the words out.

"You're going to stay with Aunt Edna just as soon as we can book you passage."

"But Mother, we had this discussion moments ago." Charlotte choked as sorrow leapt inside of her, wrapping itself around her throat until she was unable to breathe. Her mother didn't understand what she was asking of her.

Victoria snorted. "I've changed my mind."

Cold swept through her, like the jagged edge of a knife being plunged into her heart. "Mind…changed…but you can't. I told you how much I love it here," she pleaded.

"Don't cause a scene," Victoria hissed, glancing back toward the guard. "I know what you said earlier, but Egypt really isn't the proper place for a young lady. I was wrong to bring you here."

The finality in her mother's words slammed like a steel trap in Charlotte's mind. How could she think that bringing her to Egypt had been wrong? Everything good that had ever happened to her had occurred here, in this land. Charlotte didn't have any idea what she would do with herself back in London. The place seemed cold to her, unwelcoming. The rain that fell there blanketed the city in a wall of never-ending gray. She trembled even thinking about it.

"Now finish up in here, so we can be on our way." Victoria gathered her skirts and turned toward the door. Henry followed. Instead of continuing further, she halted, waiting for Charlotte.

Charlotte's stomach clenched. She felt as if she'd been struck by a blow. The storm raged on outside, while the storm inside her had already blown over. There was nothing left to say. Her mother had made up her mind. She would be packed up and carted off to London within a few days. What about Egypt? What about Ahmose? She couldn't bear to be that far away from either of them. Charlotte wasn't sure what she was going to do.

Her eyes gazed unseeing at the displays before her, as she made her way around the room. Tears pooled, threatening to spill. She was about to turn and join her parents when a sarcophagus in a corner caught her attention. She glanced over her shoulder. Her parents were still standing in the doorway, but now they were conversing with the guard. His black eyes, so much like Ahmose's, kept watching her.

Charlotte turned back to gaze at the sarcophagus. Glass surrounded it like a cage. The skin on her scalp tightened. There was no name on the plate, only information stating the Egyptologists believed the man in the case to be royalty, perhaps even a pharaoh, and had been found in Deir el-Bahari cache.

According to cartouches found with the body, he'd never married after his love vanished near the sacred waters of Karnak. Her chest tensed as the implications sunk into her mind. She stared unbelieving as her lungs labored for air. Charlotte's gaze ran from the mummy's feet, up his legs, over his shriveled waist, stopping at his chest. Her vision, blurred by the unshed tears, refused to clear. She took a ragged breath and wiped at her eyes. Charlotte blinked.

It couldn't be. No way. *Was it? Please…*

Like a brilliant rainbow of gold, the Tears of Amun shone through the dim lighting, drawing her near. Charlotte's heart slammed against her ribs. Her gaze flew to the mummy's face…sightless eyes stared back. It was Ahmose. Searing pain stabbed at her heart, ripping away the last shreds of her sanity. Her head began to spin. What was she going to do? She glanced at her parents who were now looking her way. Her mother grabbed her father's pocket watch and tapped it impatiently. Charlotte heaved air into her lungs. Her mind was racing a mile a minute.

If it worked once, would it work again? She had no way of knowing. *And what if placing the Tears of Amun around her neck didn't work?* Charlotte had no doubt she'd be arrested. They'd probably chop off her hand, and quite possibly sentence her to death considering who she would be committing the crime against. But if she didn't try she'd find herself back in London with her Aunt Edna, raising her baby alone.

Charlotte stared at her necklace, her muscles locked in place. She heard the tap of her mother's foot as her patience reached its end. Within seconds her mother would come for her and then it would be all over. Charlotte took a step forward, her mind made up. She'd rather suffer the consequences than live her life looking back and wondering "what if." Without further thought, her eyes firmly on the target, Charlotte raised her fist and smashed the glass, cutting her hand in the process.

Blood dripped onto the floor like crimson teardrops.

Her hands closed over the necklace. Slipping the clasp, she pulled it away from Ahmose. In the distance Charlotte heard her mother scream. There was a lot of shuffling of feet, but it all appeared muffled over the sound of her heartbeat. She placed the Tears of Amun on, the gold once again heavy around her neck. The air crackled as thunder burst in the sky. Charlotte turned, gazing at the scene before her.

Her father was struggling to keep the guard from rushing toward her, while her mother's hands were pressed against her cheeks in a frozen mask of outrage. Their raised voices didn't seem to reach her ears as Charlotte stared on, waiting for something to happen. The guard finally freed himself from her father's grip and rushed forward.

Nothing was happening. She was about to be arrested for stealing from the Egyptian Museum and there was absolutely nothing she could do about it.

"Sorry, Papa...I love you," Charlotte cried out to her father, who was staring at her, agog. The guard's movements seemed to slow until he appeared to be moving in reverse. Charlotte stared in fascination as he swept past her parents. The world seemed to tip on its axis and then Charlotte was falling...falling...

* * * * *

Charlotte took a deep breath and opened her eyes. She blinked twice, unable to trust her vision. She opened them again and sure enough, Ahmose's smiling face was leaning over her.

"I thought I'd lost you forever," he murmured, his voice full of pain and joy all at once.

Charlotte smiled and glanced around. She was in his palace in Thebes. "How did I get here?" she croaked, her throat parched as if she'd been lying there for days.

"You were found in Cairo by one of my servants." He brought a cup to her lips, bidding her to drink. "When you disappeared I sent everyone who could be spared out to find you." He swallowed, his black eyes misting up. "I had almost given up hope."

"Me too," she choked. "We should have remembered the inscription on the box. If we had we would never have doubted that we would be together again."

He laughed and kissed her. "Perhaps you are right. I should have recalled a fated love that must once again be." He pressed his lips to hers again, igniting the fire within her.

Charlotte gripped his shoulders, pulling him closer until his chest made contact with her aching breasts. She moaned, unable to get enough of his heat. Ahmose deepened the kiss. She slipped her hand under his kilt and began stroking his cock, reveling in the feel of his satiny hardness. His fingers tangled in her hair as he savaged her mouth. All the frustration and fear had culminated to this one moment. They needed to feel each other physically, to prove that this was real.

Charlotte grasped the belt at Ahmose's waist and tugged, while her other hand continued to pleasure him. The kilt fell to the floor.

Ahmose grabbed the linen covering her and yanked it away, revealing Charlotte's naked splendor. He released her lips and pulled away from her long enough to drink his fill, before tracing the ridges around her engorged nipples. They pebbled against his palm.

"In all the lands of Egypt, there is no beauty, such as yours." His voice was hoarse, as he choked back emotion.

"Come," she said breathlessly. "Show me."

Ahmose didn't hesitate. He slipped between Charlotte's thighs, his cock sliding over her damp pussy. He closed his eyes and groaned. "I fear I cannot wait a moment longer, my love. I must be inside you."

Charlotte tilted her hips to accommodate him. "My body awaits only you."

Ahmose positioned the head of his cock at her entrance and thrust forward. They both cried out at the exquisite torture.

"I have dreamt of this moment, since the day you vanished," he gritted out.

"My body has longed for your touch," she gasped.

"Well, wait no longer." With that Ahmose thrust again, spearing her deep.

Charlotte rose up to meet each gliding movement, her pussy gripping him in an intimate embrace. He sank inside her warmth, plunging possessively in and out, merging with her as only man and woman could. As one they moved, hot flesh upon flesh, leading each other on a journey of completion.

The familiar ache started low in her body, winding tighter and tighter. Charlotte couldn't get close enough or feel him deep enough to satisfy her endless need. After fearing she'd never hold him again, her need was desperate, urgent—frantic. She bucked her hips with each thrust of his cock, until the sensation was too much. Charlotte cried out, climaxing in a fiery explosion of ecstasy. Ahmose followed her descent into oblivion, his hips jerking as his seed spilled from his body into hers.

They lay side by side for several minutes, enjoying the intimacy. When they finally floated back down to reality, Ahmose leaned over and kissed her tenderly.

"I've got someone I'd like you to meet," she whispered against his mouth.

Ahmose braced himself on one elbow, his face quizzical.

Charlotte grabbed his hand. Slowly she brought it to her flat stomach. Ahmose frowned for but a moment then broke out into a smile that could have been seen from the heavens.

"You bring me great joy, my love." He beamed. "Just promise me one thing." Ahmose grabbed her hand and slid the gold ring she'd dropped at Karnak, back on her finger.

"What is that?"

His grin widened. "That you'll stay by my side and we'll rule the kingdoms of Egypt together."

"I promise," Charlotte laughed, slipping her hands around his neck.

"From your lips," he kissed her again, "to our son Amenhotep's ears." Ahmose leaned down and pressed his lips to her flat abdomen.

She was home.

Epilogue

ॐ

Upon the death of his brother, King Kamose, Ahmose the first became pharaoh and went on to unite the kingdoms of Egypt fulfilling his destiny. A feat, many remarked would never have occurred without his lovely wife Charlotte, the bearer of the Tears of Amun, by his side.

Their years were filled with happiness and much love, bringing into the world ten children, seven daughters and three sons. One of which, Amenhotep, would go on to become a great pharaoh, following in his father's footsteps.

Also by Jordan Summers

ও

Atlantean's Quest: The Arrival *(also available in print)*
Atlantean's Quest: Exodus *(also available in print)*
Atlantean's Quest: Redemption
Atlantean's Quest: Return
Atlantean's Quest: Atlantean Heat
Gothic Passions

About the Author

ও

I'd like to say I'm the life of the party, a laugh-a-minute kind of gal, and outrageously cool, BUT that would be a slight fabrication.

I'm actually a thirty-something, ex-flight attendant with a penchant for huge bookstores and big dumb action movies. I prefer quiet dinners with friends over maddening crowds. Happily married to my very own Highlander, we split our time between two continents.

In my spare time...LOL...I'm kidding, I don't have any spare time. The hours of my day are spent writing, and when I'm not doing that I'm thinking about writing. I guess you could say I have a one track mind.

Jordan welcomes mail from readers. You can write to her c/o Ellora's Cave Publishing at 1056 Home Avenue, Akron OH 44310-3502.

Enjoy this excerpt from:
Kieran the Black

Prologue

Kieran the Black was a notorious Norman Knight, who rumor has it, decapitated the heads of three Saxon soldiers with a single swipe of his sword—a sword that measured six and a half feet in size—the very height of the great warrior himself.

Six and a half feet! Lizzie smiled to herself and turned up the volume on the "audio tour" she had rented at the exhibition's front desk.

She, along with a dozen other journalists, had gained entrance into the coveted William the Conqueror exhibition two days before its scheduled opening to the public. Because she was a lover of all things medieval, and a member of the Society of Creative Anachronism (SCA), this assignment had been right up Lizzie's alley, and she'd jumped at the chance to attend.

Now, standing before the relics of the ultimate warrior, Kieran the Black, Lizzie's heart gave a jolt. What would it have been like to be alive in the days of men like Kieran D'Arcy—when men were six and a half feet tall, and built like brick shithouses?

"Born 1036. Died 1067. You were only thirty-one," Lizzie said aloud, resisting the urge to run a finger over the fine gothic carving of the warrior's name on the marble plaque. Something about the Norman knight stirred her soul. Perhaps because at the age of seven he had left his impoverished family to serve as page to a ruthless knight who had physically and verbally abused him. Maybe that abuse had turned Kieran's heart black, earning him the name Kieran the Black. Maybe it had given him a warrior's mentality—kill or be killed.

"Would you like to see it?"

Startled, Lizzie turned to find an old woman with frizzy white hair and enormous blue eyes standing at her side. She took off the earphones. "Sorry?"

"Would you like to see it?" The old woman nodded toward the sword encased in one-inch thick glass. "The Black One's sword."

Lizzie glanced over her shoulder. Seeing no one else about, she turned back to the woman who wore a somber black suit and crisp white blouse—similar to the employee uniforms of the exhibit hall. "Do you work here?"

The woman smiled and pushed on the glass. The side popped open on invisible hinges. Lizzie lifted her brows but remained silent as the tiny woman lifted the battle-scarred sword with little effort and put it into her suddenly damp hands.

Lizzie faltered, but held fast. The sword was heavy. So heavy, it nearly brought her to her knees, and she stood five feet, six inches tall. The woman beside her couldn't be five foot even and she had managed the sword with one hand.

Lizzie could not believe her good fortune. She wanted more than anything to have the woman take a picture of her with the treasured piece, but didn't dare ask for fear of someone seeing the flash of the camera. With her luck the exhibit hall would somehow get a hold of the photo and she and her magazine would be banned from the UK.

The woman looked directly at Lizzie, her expression serious. "The Black One was not the bad man they make him out to be."

Lizzie nodded. "I know he wasn't bad. He couldn't help what he became."

"He was a product of his time. A mercenary who lived and died by the sword."

"That's so odd that you say that. I was just thinking the same thing. He was very much a product of his time. Oh, and then to be betrayed by his best friend. Now that is wrong on so many levels." The sword felt warm in Lizzie's hands, and with every passing second grew warmer.

The woman laughed lightly. "You know of The Black One then?"

Lizzie grinned, excited to have found someone who shared her enthusiasm for the knight. "Yeah, he fascinates me. I can't explain it, but—"

"There is a rumor that if you hold the sword in your hands like so," the woman placed her hands over Lizzie's, "And rest the point of the sword on the edge of any version of Kieran's crest—see the ridge that runs right down the middle? Set the point of the sword right there—and you will be able to experience life as you've never known it."

Okay, now she was getting freaked out. Lizzie turned to the woman, who watched her expectantly. She was about to ask if she was on Candid Camera when the woman nudged her. "Go ahead…give it a try."

Lizzie glanced over both shoulders and seeing the way clear, she did as the woman asked. She set the tip of the sword on the crest, right into the ridge.

"And now?" Lizzie asked, brows lifted high, waiting for a camera crew to jump out and shout "surprise".

The woman smiled, took a step back and said, "Have a nice trip…"

Enjoy this Excerpt From:
Atlantean's Quest: The Arrival
(Book 1 of the Atlanteans Quest Series)
© Copyright Jordan Summers, 2003.

Prologue

The jungle air was thick and repressive, palpable to the taste. Like a living entity it vibrated and pulsed with an energy all its own. Animal cries rang out as predator met prey in a violent exchange that played out night after night.

A small pot set in a clearing boiled with pungent herbs and the flesh of the mighty anaconda. Steam hissed, thick fumes of smoke bellowed, wood burned, popping as each piece of kindling was snatched up by the ravenous flame.

The woman, known as Ariel the seer, stood over the crackling fire stirring the contents of the pot. Visible through the sheer material of her earthen skirt, firm muscles in her lithe legs strained. Sweat beaded her delicate brow.

With each swirling pass of the spoon, Ariel's ample breasts bobbed. Rose-colored nipples marbled from exposure to the warm night air, begging to be caressed and suckled. Long blonde hair fell in loose waves around her trim waist and over her rounded hips. Her aqua gaze fell trancelike upon the brew in search of the elusive vision.

Eros stood to the side of the seer, his massive arms crossed over his wide hairless chest, expanding his biceps to inhuman proportions. He'd braided his blond hair in the ceremonial custom of his people, divided into two plaits that fell to the small of his back. His breathing was even, despite the nervous energy coursing through his muscle-corded body, as he waited for the seer's vision to form.

Ariel gestured for Eros to come forward. *Tonight the medicine must be stronger. I need your seed to add to the brew.*

The words came into his head on a whisper. Such was the way of Atlantean communication. Unquestioning, Eros untied his loincloth, allowing it to fall away from his trim waist and thick thighs.

The night air taunted like a dream-lover's caress, promising much, delivering little. A faint breeze spilled over his rod, rustling the crisp curls that grew at the base. He reached down to take himself in hand, but the seer stopped his movement with a light touch of her fingertips.

I must be the one who brings your seed forth this night, for the ritual to be complete.

Eros nodded and dropped his hands to his sides. The seer stepped forward and cupped his heavy sac in her soft palms, transferring his weight back and forth until balance was achieved. Her gentle touch brought forth the desired results. His staff hardened, lengthening to its full ten inches within seconds.

At once, she slipped to her knees impaling her mouth with his throbbing cock. Her lips were hot, moist, made for giving pleasure. He sucked in a breath, but said nothing. Ariel began swirling her tongue around the head of his staff, like she'd done so many times before when he'd sought relief. Her hands gently massaged his balls, supping at him as if he were her first meal after a long starvation.

Eros gave his body up to the pleasurable sensation and closed his eyes, imagining what it would feel like to thrust into his future mate. Like a siren of the sea, the warmth of the seer's mouth urged, beckoned, and lured the seed from him. He felt his sac draw up as Ariel added pressure and switched to sucking, sliding her hand up and down his thick cock.

As he started to ejaculate, Ariel pulled away, ensuring he spilled his essence into the strange mixture bubbling within the pot. Eros jerked as the last of his fluids were milked from his body.

Ariel returned to the pot and stirred a couple more times. Her eyes intense, focused, waiting.

Excitement filled her mind, spilling over into Eros. *She comes, my King. Her arrival heralds the new dawn of our people.*

Eros lowered his gaze in respect. *Are you certain?* He normally never questioned the seer, yet tonight he had no choice. Her vision must be true.

For his sake. For the sake of his people.

Ariel hesitated, clearing the smoke from around the gurgling pot with a wave of her slender hand. *'Tis true. She will arrive within seven moonrises. 'Tis more than enough time to bring her here and perform the mating ritual. Remember, you must not join with her until the ceremony has been completed.*

Aye, he answered silently.

Wait. She stilled, her eyes widened a bit and her breath caught. *You must use caution, for she does not travel alone.*

Eros stiffened, rage coursing through his body. *Do you see her with a mate*?

The seer's mouth held the trace of a smile. His heart pounded painfully against his ribcage. It should not matter to him whether the woman had chosen a mate, but the ice forming in his veins said it did.

Nay. Ariel shook her head. *But she is in danger from one who is very near.*

His stomach clenched. His hands fisted so tight he half expected to hear bones breaking. *I will not allow any harm to come to her.*

Eros raised his head to the heavens. After all the waiting, his mate was finally coming. He had almost given up hope. But tonight Ariel had seen her. He could barely believe his good fortune.

Soon, he too would lay eyes on his future mate. Until then, there was much to do.

All is as it should be. Eros looked into the seer's face and nodded. *You have done your part, now 'tis time for me to do mine. Be well, Ariel the seer.* He dropped to his knees before her, kissing each bare nipple reverently as was custom, then rose and slipped into the darkness.

Be well, my King.

* * * * *

Rachel was back in the jungle—naked. Monkeys chattered and parrots screeched as she lay on a soft bed of grass in the small clearing. The blades tickled her bottom and stroked her shoulders as a breeze gently rustled them. Water gurgled and splashed playfully in the background, calling out for those around to join in its merriment. She considered answering its call, but she couldn't seem to sit up. The smell of exotic orchids wafted on the breeze, perfuming the air, bathing her skin with their luscious scent.

Suddenly all sound stopped. Even the leaves refused to whisper.

Rachel's heart began to pound, a combination of excitement and fear. Her rosy nipples stabbed skyward.

He was here.

Silent footfalls heralded his approach. Shadows from the trees shifted like a mirage as he strode toward her. Flawlessly muscled, his body chiseled perfection.

Rachel gasped and tried to get a glimpse of his face, but before she could do so, a strange shadowy light filtered over him obscuring his features.

She knew she should scream, but the sight of this stranger's body and his mammoth cock made her mouth water, her legs tremble, and her pussy ache.

It had been far too long since she'd had a man, and she *wanted* this one, more than she wanted her next breath. She raised her arms to reach for him, but he pulled back.

Rachel cursed.

The man kneeled between her thighs and pressed them apart, exposing her pussy. The shadows around his face refused to budge. He lowered his head and lapped at her swollen folds. Every nerve ending came alive, as his seeking tongue sent shockwaves through her body. She was already wet. A thin sheen of perspiration broke out on her skin, her nipples puckered even tighter until they ached. Rachel moaned, low and deep—animal-like.

Fuck me, please, she begged in her mind as she attempted to shift her hips.

He did not answer.

She heard his labored breath as he rose and positioned the head of his great cock at her entrance. He smelled of earth, spice and sex incarnate. A heady human aphrodisiac of male testosterone and primal urges. Rachel bucked her hips, nudging, encouraging, and pleading for his thick length. Didn't he realize how much she needed him?

He groaned. His large frame shook as if grasping for control.

She felt the pain-pressure as he started to push the tip of his thick erection inside, stretching her body beyond its limits. The moisture from her channel eased his way. Rachel whimpered, trying to find the words to ask for what she needed, but before a single syllable was uttered he vanished.

"Noooo!" The scream died on Rachel's lips as she jackknifed up in her bed. She blinked a couple of times and her apartment came into focus. Her body was drenched and her breathing ragged. The sheets were twisted around her ankles, effectively binding her to the bed. She looked around her studio apartment. The man was gone and her clit ached.

She'd been having the same erotic dream every night for the past month. Shadowy, elusive—downright frustrating, like the man in it. Rachel snorted and shook her head. She thought about him as if he were real.

She kicked the covers away and threw her legs over the side of the bed. Rachel padded into the bathroom, her bare feet echoing off the hardwood floors. There was no way she could go back to sleep without a good orgasm.

The buzz of her vibrator and her own soft moans rang out in the night's silence as she brought herself to climax while she imagined being fucked by the jungle god...

Why an electronic book?

We live in the Information Age—an exciting time in the history of human civilization, in which technology rules supreme and continues to progress in leaps and bounds every minute of every day. For a multitude of reasons, more and more avid literary fans are opting to purchase e-books instead of paper books. The question from those not yet initiated into the world of electronic reading is simply: *Why?*

1. ***Price.*** An electronic title at Ellora's Cave Publishing and Cerridwen Press runs anywhere from 40% to 75% less than the cover price of the exact same title in paperback format. Why? Basic mathematics and cost. It is less expensive to publish an e-book (no paper and printing, no warehousing and shipping) than it is to publish a paperback, so the savings are passed along to the consumer.

2. ***Space.*** Running out of room in your house for your books? That is one worry you will never have with electronic books. For a low one-time cost, you can purchase a handheld device specifically designed for e-reading. Many e-readers have large, convenient screens for viewing. Better yet, hundreds of titles can be stored within your new library—on a single microchip. There are a variety of e-readers from different manufacturers. You can also read e-books on your PC or laptop computer. (Please note that Ellora's

Cave does not endorse any specific brands. You can check our websites at www.ellorascave.com or www.cerridwenpress.com for information we make available to new consumers.)

3. *Mobility*. Because your new e-library consists of only a microchip within a small, easily transportable e-reader, your entire cache of books can be taken with you wherever you go.

4. ***Personal Viewing Preferences.*** Are the words you are currently reading too small? Too large? Too… ANNOYING? Paperback books cannot be modified according to personal preferences, but e-books can.

5. ***Instant Gratification.*** Is it the middle of the night and all the bookstores near you are closed? Are you tired of waiting days, sometimes weeks, for bookstores to ship the novels you bought? Ellora's Cave Publishing sells instantaneous downloads twenty-four hours a day, seven days a week, every day of the year. Our webstore is never closed. Our e-book delivery system is 100% automated, meaning your order is filled as soon as you pay for it.

Those are a few of the top reasons why electronic books are replacing paperbacks for many avid readers.

As always, Ellora's Cave and Cerridwen Press welcome your questions and comments. We invite you to email us at Comments@ellorascave.com or write to us directly at Ellora's Cave Publishing Inc., 1056 Home Avenue, Akron, OH 44310-3502.

THE
☥ ELLORA'S CAVE ☥
LIBRARY

Stay up to date with Ellora's Cave Titles in
Print with our Quarterly Catalog.

TO RECIEVE A CATALOG,
SEND AN EMAIL WITH YOUR NAME
AND MAILING ADDRESS TO:

CATALOG@ELLORASCAVE.COM

OR SEND A LETTER OR POSTCARD
WITH YOUR MAILING ADDRESS TO:

CATALOG REQUEST
C/O ELLORA'S CAVE PUBLISHING, INC.
1056 HOME AVENUE
AKRON, OHIO 44310-3502